ALPACA LIES

ELLEN RIGGS

Alpaca Lies

Copyright © 2020 Ellen Riggs

ISBN 978-1-989303-61-0 eBook
ISBN 978-1-989303-60-3 Book
ASIN B088P4PS84 Kindle
ASIN TBD Paperback
Publisher: Ellen Riggs

www.ellenriggs.com
Cover designer: Lou Harper
Editor: Serena Clarke
2010072336

CHAPTER ONE

Alvina, the woolly brown alpaca, skipped joyfully along the fence inside her pasture. She did a double twirl, followed by a series of hops and then a buck. The sequence ended with a reverse spin and a double buck, after which she stood, head high and legs splayed, waiting for well-earned applause.

Clapping hard, I turned to Jilly Blackwood, my best friend. "She's outdone herself, hasn't she? That's an entirely new combination."

"Bravo," Jilly called, clapping too. She was wearing a black knit dress topped by a cashmere coat and a long pale blue scarf, also cashmere. As a headhunter in Boston, she'd built a vast collection of cashmere that served her well here at Runaway Farm now that winter was breathing down our necks. Like me, however, she felt somewhat conflicted over wearing—or devouring—animal products. Farm life had thrown plenty of our city girl assumptions into question, but it also kept us too busy for much rumination.

Alvina ignored Jilly and me. Instead, her beautiful big brown eyes were trained on my brother, the current love of her life. Asher didn't take that honor for granted. On the contrary, he was puffing from the effort of proving himself worthy. Alvina only danced when motivated by a human partner, and while Asher's moves looked more like a CrossFit workout, complete with lunges and burpees, I could see how each observed and inspired the other. It was an endearing cross-species partnership.

Tall, fair and blue-eyed, Asher flashed his trademark grin at his camelid admirer. "Well done, sweetheart," he called to Alvina. "You are so wasted here with these sad sacks." He gestured to the pair of llamas huddled in the corner of the pasture with their trio of guard donkeys. Drama Llama, the tallest of the herd, gave my brother a baleful glance. As much as Alvina loved Asher for his flashy moves, Drama despised him. In fact, I'd barred Asher from entering the pasture after Drama escaped and took a bead on Keats, my brilliant sheepdog. That move had landed the feisty llama in the same category as Wilma the sly sow: hooved and dangerous. Well, technically llamas had toes, but it sounded better that way.

Before moving to Runaway Farm in quaint Clover Grove a few months ago, I'd expected all the animals to be calm and cooperative. Those were city girl delusions, as it turned out. The livestock primarily consisted of rescues that had been neglected, abused or both. As a result, they were quirky and unpredictable. I still hoped to win them over eventually, but for now all I could do was try to avoid getting chomped, trampled or squished.

"Hey. Galloway!" The shout made me jump. "That behavior is unbecoming of an officer of the law."

Kellan Harper, the chief of police and also my boyfriend, had arrived unnoticed during the Asher-Alvina show. He strolled across the gravel parking area to join us at the fence, looking even hotter in civvies than he did in uniform. My heart did a few crazy hops in greeting, similar to the moves of the pygmy goats in their pen nearby.

"I'm off duty, Chief," Asher called back, still puffing and grinning. "And don't knock it till you've tried it."

Kellan kissed my cheek and then dusted his black wool coat with one hand. It was a losing battle. Within seconds of leaving his SUV his clothes were always covered in fur, fluff and feathers. He couldn't do much about his uniforms but he'd have to rethink his casual wardrobe if he continued to date me. His dry cleaner was charging a premium to remove embedded fibers and darn the holes in pant cuffs left by Keats during his herding drills.

The black-and-white dog had crouched behind Jilly to stage an ambush. His warm brown eye gleamed with fun, while the blue eye was coolly intent on his prey. As a complete animal novice, Kellan was the perfect target. Despite being a decorated detective and the youngest chief of police in the entire state, he couldn't wrap his head around this ongoing siege from a sheepdog. Worse, Percy, my marmalade cat, had joined the game and was skulking along the top rung of the fence toward Kellan. The bright fluff was hard to miss, yet Kellan missed it. Percy launched first with his new signature move: a bounce off Kellan's broad shoulders. As the cat landed lightly on the near-frozen ground, Keats moved in for a quick nip before the two animals darted away.

Kellan jumped and uttered what might have been called a squeal in a lesser man.

Jilly covered her mouth and turned away, but Asher doubled over with laughter. "Boss, you just screamed like a girl. I saw air under your feet."

"Never mind, Asher," I said, hooking my arm through Kellan's. "Keats, Percy, behave yourselves."

The dastardly duo had disappeared around the barn, so my rebuke was futile.

"Honestly, Ivy," Kellan said, disengaging his arm so that he could brush dusty paw prints off his shoulder. "Why can't they pick on Asher?"

"Golden boy," I said, shrugging. "Always has been."

Mom said Asher was born smiling, and more than a decade of police work hadn't wiped the grin off his face. After falling hard for Jilly, he had even more to beam over. It was no wonder Alvina favored my brother over me, no matter how many treats I offered. Asher had a lightness of spirit that attracted everyone.

Of all of us, Asher was the least affected by the recent spate of murders on or near Runaway Farm. Like me, Jilly was thinner and paler than when she arrived to help me get the inn launched. But we hung in there. With every catastrophe, it seemed we became more committed to this place, to our friendship and to our expanding community of loved ones. Jilly was only marginally more interested in animals than Kellan but every day they grew on her a little.

Especially Keats. My genius sheepdog now communicated with Jilly as well as me in his strange mumble talk. If her guard was down, she even answered him out loud. Afterward, she turned bright red, knowing we'd become a cast of oddballs. That didn't bother me much anymore. Listening to Keats and studying his behavior and signals had saved my hide plenty of times. Percy brought valuable insights, too, from a feline perspective.

With the way people were dying around Clover Grove, I needed to keep an open mind. If it took learning the language of every creature here to stay ahead of the curve, I was up for the challenge. My brain wasn't as sharp as it had been before the concussion I sustained rescuing Keats, yet every day it seemed like my neurons rewired in innovative ways that suited my new life. For a decade, I was a human resources exec known as the "grim reaper" for my talent in downsizing people and destroying their lives. Now I was a hobby farmer and innkeeper who talked aloud to her animals and helped solve murders when the need arose.

The need kept arising, much to Kellan's dismay. Maybe we were done now. How long could a string of bad luck go on?

"Golden Boy," Jilly called. "You'll lose your luster if we don't get to your mom's recital on time."

"Do we have to?" Asher's perma-smile contracted slightly. "Can't we say something came up? Something always comes up here."

"True, but this is important to Dahlia," Jilly said. "And you love dancing."

"I love dancing with you," he said. "And Alvina, my other girlfriend."

Jilly flushed. They'd only squeezed in a dozen dates between getting the inn running and solving murders but she didn't argue. Asher's relentless optimism and sheer decency were steadily winning her over. Like me, she'd been jaded by her previous career, and the crimes we'd seen since our move hadn't exactly restored her faith in humanity. It was hard for her to trust that Asher was the real deal but they'd get there. Some day soon, I predicted she'd make him her special Fall-in-Love Beef Stroganoff and the rest would be history.

Kellan stopped brushing at his coat and grimaced. "Ballroom dancing isn't really our thing, ladies. We're cops, remember?"

"You're very light on your feet," I said. "Elegant, actually. I'd bet you'd make a fine—"

He directed his palm at me. "Ivy, don't."

"That's a direct hit to his masculinity," Jilly said, wagging an index finger at me. "Have I taught you nothing?"

"I don't speak your language," I said, laughing. "Try translating into canine and I might get it."

Turning, I snapped my fingers at Keats and Percy, who'd reappeared and begun stalking each other blatantly. It was a game of chicken to see who'd break first.

"Keats," Jilly called. "Herd everyone into Kellan's car, please. We're losing the light, and I, for one, am excited to see this performance. I'm even more excited for the reception, where we can hand out some business cards. Ivy, we're selling, remember?"

I sighed. When the farm and nearly-finished inn practically fell into my lap, thanks to heiress Hannah Pemberton, I hadn't realized I'd need to promote all the time. That didn't come easily to me, but guests didn't come easily either. Hannah had expected the upscale "farm experience" to sell itself, and it probably would have... for her. No one had died on her watch.

Asher reached over the fence to pat Alvina's neck. He murmured sweet nothings and she hummed back in yet another form of interspecies communication. Then he turned and loped toward us. His eyes were on my pretty blonde friend, which is why he didn't notice the big heap of manure in his path. Charlie had been exercising Florence, the mare, on a long line earlier and missed a flap.

"Look sharp!" My warning came too late. Asher went down as if in slow motion. His arms pinwheeled and one leg kicked out theatrically. Inside the pasture, Alvina combined a leap and a spin in response.

Jilly ran over to him and I marvelled as always at how well she maneuvered in heels on uneven ground. "Are you all right?" she asked.

"Yeah, yeah." He waved her away. Asher didn't flush often but having his lady love try to help him out of a nasty skid brought color to his cheeks.

I could barely stop laughing long enough to echo her words. "Jilly, you're emasculating him. Have I taught you nothing?"

Keats joined them and took little lunges at Asher to get him moving.

"Fine," Jilly said. "But stink or no stink, we are going to that recital. Your mom is doing her part to bring a little culture back to this town and deserves our support."

Asher clambered to his feet and came toward me, crusty hands outstretched like a zombie. "Stop laughing, little sister, or I'll eat your brain."

I ran toward the car, not doing nearly as well on heels as Jilly. My natural clumsiness had only gotten worse after the head injury.

"Don't you dare touch her, Asher Galloway," Jilly called, gesturing for Keats to corral him and flicking her fingers toward the house. "Ivy and I have to sell the farm experience while you two stand around being impressive cops."

"Being impressive isn't as easy as it looks," Kellan said, smirking. "Especially when you stink."

Keats circled my brother and herded him inside. Alvina stood at the fence staring after Asher and bleating mournfully. Turning, I dodged Jilly and went back to the alpaca. I tried to comfort her with a pat but she moved out of reach. Running back, Keats wedged himself between us to ease me away. Forcing myself on Alvina or the llamas usually ended with my getting spit on. The semi-digested green goop smelled far worse than manure and stained terribly.

"One day you're going to love me, girl," I said, allowing

Keats to guide me away. He nudged my hand to reassure me that he saw my charms, even if the camelids did not.

"They don't all need to love you," Kellan said, offering his arm with a smile that could melt the heels off a girl's feet. "Keats and I got you covered."

Jilly opened the driver's door and gestured. "Stop smoldering, Chief, and get inside. The tango awaits."

CHAPTER TWO

The yoga studio looked the same as it had when Jilly and I visited a couple of months ago to interview the previous owner. He'd gone out of business and left town after obstructing the investigation into dogcatcher Lloyd Boyce's death, and now the attractive space hosted far different classes.

We hung up our coats and lined up with everyone else against the wall, forced out front by our tardy arrival. The vast mirrors reflected my discomfort as dance instructor José Batista propelled Mom around the room. Their heels clicked sharply on the gleaming hardwood floors and Mom looked just as enthusiastic as Alvina had earlier. Then José swept her into a deep dip right in front of her six adult children, lined up in the front row.

Nearly everyone in the audience of more than 30 people gasped as Mom's backcombed bouffant dusted the floor. Some gasps sounded like horror and others like admiration. The noises coming from my siblings were harder to pinpoint.

It took a lot for Mom to embarrass us now. We were used to her antics, and ballroom dancing was nothing compared to her propensity for running down stop signs in Buttercup, her old yellow sedan. Asher had been ordered by Kellan to confiscate her license after the pile of traffic violations threatened to bury our petite mother, if not other citizens.

"Maybe he'll drop her," my sister Poppy whispered, louder than necessary. She considered herself the rebel of the family and showed it by dyeing the dark hair we Galloway Girls shared royal blue or purple. "One more spin and she'll go flying."

Mom was tiny and fit, and it did seem like José was exploiting that in his demonstration. He raised her arm and sent her into a pirouette that made her red sequinned chiffon skirt flare. Mom had sworn never to wear chiffon, let alone sequins. Tonight she was one pair of skates short of the Ice Capades.

I had to hand it to her, though. Unlike so many Clover Grove women of her generation, Dahlia Galloway embraced change. That had always been true, at least since my father had left her with six kids to raise on her own. She'd cycled through a series of low-paying jobs, getting fired for a variety of issues. As an HR exec, I had decided Mom was ill-suited to work of any kind. She was a gadabout, a social butterfly—a perpetually whirring ruby-throated hummingbird in her signature red dresses. Nothing and no one held her interest for long, not even her own children.

That's why I feared for the future of Bloomers, the unisex salon she'd recently launched with my sister, Iris. There was no denying that Mom seemed to have found her calling as a barber, however. Men were flocking to the salon for her classic straightedge shave—even after she'd briefly been accused of murder by sharp object. It wasn't the first time she'd been accused of murder, or even the second. Mom was quick with a quip and a sharp word that could be taken as a legitimate threat. Kellan and I had our work cut out for us in clearing her name, but maybe her twin passions for barbering and ballroom dance would finally soften her edges.

"How long is this going to last?" Asher whispered. "It's worse than the time I wrestled that alligator in a ditch and—"

The last words never emerged, likely because Jilly pinched them off.

"There are no 'gators in Clover Grove," Poppy said. "Unless Ivy's rescued one."

"There was," Asher insisted. "An escaped exotic. Mom turned it into those shoes."

"Stop it, you two," Jilly hissed. She glared at them and then shared it around to the rest of us. Perhaps she sensed the hysterical laughter bubbling up in my throat. For some reason, Jilly and Mom had really hit it off. Keats was fond of Mom, too, which said something because his inner circle of unstalkable people was quite small.

Kellan's big hand released mine and slid up to my elbow. It wasn't meant to be flirtatious but it still sent small shocks pinging toward my heart. Our fire ignited in high school, and despite a 10-year gap, continued to smoke. Now, he was just trying to keep me from lapsing into helpless giggles that would trigger the entire family. Judging by the way the men in the crowd were covering their mouths and clearing their throats, we'd have plenty of company.

"It's a big moment for your mother. Let her shine," Kellan whispered, before pressing his lips firmly together. He was a master of the poker face. That was in the job description for the chief of police. Sometimes he looked as impassive as a mannequin.

His restraint had a calming effect on the rest of us and we stared at our feet, casting furtive glances at each other.

Soon, the gurgle of laughter eased down my throat to

churn in my stomach. That's when I started sensing a strange vibe in the room. The hair on my arms prickled and it wasn't a reaction to Kellan's touch. If Keats were here, instead of waiting in the car, his hackles would be up. I relied on the dog to confirm my feelings, but I was coming to trust my own intuition, too. After my concussion, many of my suspicions seemed paranoid and delusional. Then people started dying. Paying attention to those thoughts had become the sage thing to do.

"What's wrong?" Kellan asked. His intuition was also well honed from years of detective work in Philadelphia before returning to the supposed peace of his quaint hometown.

"Not sure. Something's just not right." The fingers of my free hand twitched at my side, longing to feel my dog's pricked ears. "I need Keats."

"You'll have to settle for the chief of police." He leaned in and his deep voice buzzed in my ear. "Keats has fangs but I'm packing heat."

My hand shot up to my mouth to smother the giggle and now Jilly treated Kellan to a glare as well. She wasn't in the least intimidated by him. Her old job of dealing with business titans made her confident and contained.

Finally, after what seemed like an interminable routine, José took a deep bow. Then he swung Mom around and she curtsied till red chiffon brushed the floor. As if that weren't enough, José spun her again and dipped her. She kicked up a red pump as punctuation. They held that pose for so long everyone started shifting.

"Chief," Asher said. "Can you shoot me now? You promised to take me out if—"

"Officer Galloway," Kellan said. "Shut it."

"Me first," Poppy said. "If there's an encore, I'm going to do something desperate."

"We're already standing," Iris said. "Maybe we should sit down."

"Don't you dare." Daisy, the eldest and unofficial matriarch, sounded horrified. "There are no chairs."

Her cheeks were splotchy from stress and I knew she was relieved she'd left her kids—two sets of twin teenage boys—at home. She had her hands full with her sibling "children."

"Just stop clapping," I said. "We've done the polite thing. Any more applause will encourage them."

Too late. The music started again, and this time it was something very sensual. José's legs twisted through Mom's and there wasn't enough space between them for a puff of air. In fact, the entire studio seemed airless and my hand clutched at my throat.

"Ivy. Ivy?" Kellan's voice sounded far away. I felt his arm drop around me and we moved through the crowd, although my feet didn't get the order. Kellan half-carried me downstairs and out into the street, where I pulled in deep, frosty gusts of the late fall air.

"Thank you," I said, leaning into him. "That was close."

"Are you telling me the fearless woman who faces down murderers collapses in the face of the rhumba?"

"Don't say it," I pleaded. "Even the memory makes me queasy. But it was more than my mom getting up close and personal with a virtual stranger. There was a bad vibe in that room. Couldn't you feel it?"

He waited a beat before nodding. "Something felt off. But not enough to faint over."

"I get claustrophobic after my accident. That's why I take Keats everywhere." I followed Jilly's normal direction of breathing in for five and out for five. "Mom banned him tonight, and I was afraid he'd get crushed in there anyway."

"Who would have expected such a turnout for a dance recital?" Kellan asked.

"Hazel Bingham says we're culture-starved as a town." I let him prop me against the building so that he could shrug off his sports jacket. "This seems to support her claim."

Hazel was one of our oldest and most distinguished residents and we'd hit it off right away when we met recently. She remembered a time when Clover Grove embraced art, music and theater, among other pursuits. Now the town revolved around homesteading. The only classes I'd seen advertised were for gardening, preserving and the perpetually popular Happy Hens seminar. We'd gone so far back to our agricultural roots, Hazel said, that we had "all the vibrance of potatoes."

"If the rhumba is culture, I'll stick with being— Well, whatever I am," Kellan said, slipping his jacket around my shoulders.

"What you are is wonderfully brave for seeing the Galloways through one of the most stressful moments of our life as a family," I said, kissing his chin. I was the tallest of the Galloway Girls and it was nice to have a man to reach up to.

"More stressful than repeated murder investigations?" he asked, eyebrows rising.

"Oh, much. One murder is pretty much the same as the next once you've been through it," I said, smiling.

He shook his head but smiled, too. "I've never found that to be true. And I have a few more murders under my belt than you."

I pushed off the wall and tugged on his hand. "Let's leave it that way, shall we? I'm ready to retire from the murder business and run my tranquil inn."

"Sounds perfect to me." He followed reluctantly. "Where are we going?"

"To get Keats. There's no way I'm going back in there without him."

"We have to go back? Why? We paid our respects and you nearly fainted."

"There's a reception," I said. "With sandwiches."

"I don't want a sandwich." It was as close to a whine as he ever got. "You know what happens at events like this. People hit me up over every little complaint 'off the record.' A neighbor's fence is too high. Someone else has too many chickens. And then there's the guy who runs his leaf blower too early on Sunday mornings. No amount of tuna salad is worth it."

"Trust me, I know." I forged on to Kellan's SUV, where Keats' blue eye gleamed from the driver's window.

"He's in my seat," Kellan said. "Isn't that a little presumptuous?"

I shrugged. "You're not using it right now."

"So I've got to compete with a sheepdog for the rest of my life?"

Sparks ran up my spine again. Words like "the rest of my life" did that to me, coming from Kellan. Especially when his furry competitor and I routinely interfered with his police work. Well, I didn't see them as being in competition. They complemented each other and formed a perfect backup team for me, along with Jilly. I'd like to say my family was part of that team, but the jury was still out. I hadn't missed them much during my decade in Boston, but since coming home they were growing on me. More like a fungus than a sweet trailing vine, but growing nonetheless. Even Mom.

After I let him out, Keats frisked around us like a carefree puppy. It was good to see, because he'd never actually *been* a carefree puppy, or at least not for long. Once I'd rescued him from a criminal, he could have kicked back and had an easy life, but it wasn't in his makeup. He was a working dog with a farm to manage. Even when he wasn't on the job, he kept busy solving crimes or practicing his stealth moves on Kellan, as he was now.

"Leave it, Keats," I said. "The chief deserves better for putting up with us." I looped my arm through Kellan's and we started back to the studio. "In fact, the man deserves a nice sandwich. And if you could keep the pesky complainers away, maybe Kellan would like you."

"Oh, I like Keats well enough," Kellan said. "Even more if he'd stop herding me."

"Tonight he can herd away others while I work the room. I promised Jilly I'd hand out some cards and I can't let her down. We can't keep the inn going without some warm bodies."

"It's the cold bodies that are causing you trouble," Kellan said, as we walked toward the entrance arm in arm. "That's what we need to fix."

I stopped a few yards before the door. "No murder talk, okay? And if you don't mind, I'd rather mingle on my own. I'm embarrassed to be flogging my wares in front of you."

"In other words, the police chief's presence shuts people down," he said, grinning.

"Have I told you you're amazing tonight?" I asked.

"Can't hear it often enough."

He was about to lean over and kiss me when the studio door burst open and a woman ran out. She was a middle-aged brunette I couldn't remember seeing before. When I noticed she was crying, I pulled Kellan against the wall to give her some privacy. She was so busy patting her eyes with tissues that I doubted she noticed us.

"Strange," Kellan said, looking after her. "I didn't find the performance that moving."

I looked at Keats and his tail and ears had drooped. "Told you. Bad vibes in that room. I hope she's okay."

"Well, she didn't wait around to be asked," he said, nudging me inside. "So let's get this over with, shall we?"

I nodded. "I hope all culture isn't this painful. Or we'll be crying, too."

CHAPTER THREE

Jilly beckoned and I joined her with Keats. She'd given Asher the slip, too, so that we could mingle more freely. We started small, with Teri Mason, the artist who owned Hill Country Designs, and Mabel Halliday, who owned Miniature Mutts, the ceramics store. I considered both to be friends, something that still surprised me. I'd never had time nor inclination for friends in Boston. Jilly had filled all the roles in my life, which wasn't entirely fair to her. No doubt she was secretly glad to be shifting some of the load for my emotional welfare to Keats, Kellan and others.

Mabel was slightly plump and attractive with a classic, highlighted bob. Her husband, Alf, matched her perfectly, also being round and fair. He'd recently started helping Mabel in her store and she'd said it was a mixed blessing. Income was up and marital bliss down. She loved running her own little kingdom, surrounded by tiny ceramic dogs, houses and farm animals. I wasn't into ceramics as a rule, but when I passed Mabel's store I eyed her Christmas village display with childlike awe.

Teri and Mabel had creativity in common but the resemblance ended there. With a shock of multicolored hair that left Poppy's in the dust, and a bohemian caftan, Teri definitely looked the part of the artist. I loved her work, especially the realistic yet whimsical portrait she'd done of Keats that had pride of place over my mantel. She'd captured the essence of my special dog, and it seemed as if Keats himself knew that, because the white tuft of his tail gave Teri the swish of approval.

When she pulled a tall man forward, however, Keats' tail drifted down. Either he didn't like the man, or he didn't like Teri's attention being diverted.

"Ivy, this is my friend Kevin Breen," Teri said. The color in her cheeks told me that Kevin was more than a friend. I was happy for her, because it wasn't easy to meet eligible men in a small town. I had three single sisters to prove that. Hazel Bingham complained that all the "quality" men left for jobs in the city, and my casual observation suggested she wasn't far wrong. I secretly hoped I could attract some good ones as guests at the inn and introduce them to Iris and Violet. Poppy would never fall for that. Her misadventures in dating seemed likely to continue as long as she had breath to offend people.

Kevin Breen was polite, soft-spoken and reasonably attractive, but he seemed far too conservative for Teri. Opposites surely did attract, however. Kellan and I were proof of that. Jilly and Asher weren't similar either, aside from being fair and exceptionally attractive.

Keats remained unimpressed with Kevin and when Teri noticed his tail was down, her brows came together and I discreetly excused myself. There was no need to dampen her enthusiasm with the judgments of a sheepdog. That said, I worried for her. Keats didn't normally do a blatant tail drop without good reason.

The tail stayed down when we bumped into Simon Rezek, owner of Grub, the local feed store. I liked Simon, with his crazy gray curls, twinkling blue eyes, and wide smile. In fact, everyone liked Simon. He was the guy you could count on for casual advice on everything from a lame horse to a gassy cow to a hen that wouldn't lay. In fact, he ran the Happy Hens seminar when the regular instructor was out of commission.

"Hey, buddy," Simon said, trying to pat Keats and looking puzzled as my dog backed away. "What gives? All dogs like me."

"It's not about you," I said. "It's about Gregor."

Every time we dropped by Grub, Simon's huge brindle mastiff took issue with Keats. While Keats normally didn't let other dogs faze him, the mastiff's sheer size and ferocity couldn't be ignored. I'd started leaving Keats in the car, which he resented, because the feed store was full of amazing smells.

"Aw, come on," Simon said. "Keats, you just need to suck up a little to Gregor. He's a pussycat when you curtsy."

I laughed. "Keats curtsies to no one, I'm afraid. His secret weapon is indifference but Gregor isn't falling for it."

"Dogs will be dogs," Simon said, shrugging broad shoulders. "They've all got their personalities, just like us."

Anne Rezek, Simon's wife, came up behind him with a plate piled high with sandwiches. Taking a peanut butter and banana pinwheel, he stuffed it into his mouth whole and grinned at her expression.

"Oh honey, we're in public," Anne said, shaking her head. Unlike Mom, Anne had grown her silver gossamer hair long. Her eyes were as blue as her husband's and her face had few lines. Also unlike Mom, Anne was conservative—even demure. Tonight she wore a periwinkle blue dress that probably came off the racks from Chez Belle, the town's only designer.

"Speaking of curtsies," Simon said, after washing down the sandwich with the small cup of punch his wife offered. "That was some number your mom did with... what's his name?"

"José," Anne and I said at once, and then laughed.

"Wow, that guy really makes an impression." Simon reached for another sandwich. "What's his secret? Everyone who comes into the store is chattering about him."

"Got me," I said, glancing across the room. José wasn't anything special, at least to my eye. He was slight and a little slick, with hair in a long wispy pigtail that looked awfully dark for a man in his fifties. If Mom was dating him—a distinct possibility—she was probably working her salon magic. She had what she described as a "rotation" of men who were more than happy to show her all that Clover Grove and surrounding towns had to offer. "I guess José's got the moves. He's a little more exotic than most of the men around here."

Anne tossed her silvery hair. "Not to my taste. But I've never cared for dancing, either. Too frivolous."

"Same," I said. "Although I'm all for more frivolous pursuits in Clover Grove. Hazel Bingham is trying to revive the town's former culture and Jilly and I are going to open up the inn to new groups."

"We don't have time for culture," Simon said. "The store keeps us busy. Livestock are hungry year-round."

"True enough," I said. "But we'll keep trying to lure you out."

Simon smirked. "I'd rather get dragged by a bull than attend art appreciation night."

"Oh, honey," Anne said, smiling up at her tall husband. "Have another sandwich."

Jilly beckoned and Keats and I joined her. She was talking to Ryan Snopes, the owner of Peachtree Fine Foods, a small, upscale grocer in town. Ryan had played football with Asher in high school, and while fine dining had added some bulk in the years since, he was still an attractive man with an army style crew cut courtesy of Mom's razor. He'd had the good sense to follow the trends in Clover Grove and converted what had been little more than a convenience store into the destination of choice for passionate foodies like Jilly. There were more of them around than I expected. Sometimes I waited outside with Keats while Jilly and other customers discussed recipes and ingredients. I was glad she'd found her tribe and there was no reason to let my boredom ruin her good time.

Tonight Ryan was with Tish Ramsey, his girlfriend, who was nearly a decade behind me in school. Her flaming red hair, green eyes and pale freckled skin made her hard to miss in a room dominated by older women.

"Wasn't your mother amazing?" Tish said, smiling. I was surprised to see she was wearing braces. Her teeth had always looked good to me, but most did after examining the worn, yellowed choppers of various ruminants.

"Mom frequently amazes me," I said. "This was definitely unexpected."

"She's José's star student in our class," Tish continued. "Has she taken lessons before?"

"Not to my knowledge, but she's a woman of mystery."

"Well, if she's a natural, she's very gifted." Tish paused before quietly adding, "Or maybe she's getting private lessons."

I reeled back at the implication and Jilly gave my sleeve a

little jerk to keep me from saying anything I shouldn't. It was certainly possible that Mom was spending extra time with José, but if so, he had plenty of competition. Mom didn't invest much time in any one man. The whole point of a rotation, she said, was to keep anyone from getting attached. Her goal was to stay footloose and fancy free, and I didn't see that changing any time soon.

Jilly took a small step forward, just enough to put Tish on notice. "Dahlia's naturally graceful. It doesn't surprise me at all that she'd take the dance floor by storm."

"She's a performer at heart," I chimed in. "Maybe she's finally found her stage."

Tish flashed her braces in a sly smile. "Some of the ladies are a little jealous, that's all." She glanced at her boyfriend. "Not me, of course."

A flicker of annoyance crossed Ryan's normally placid face as he stared across the room at José. "I don't get it. It's all 'José this and José that' when ladies come into the store these days. He doesn't look that great, but what do I know?"

"It's the way he moves," Tish said. Her eyes lost focus for a second and her voice had a dreamy lilt. "He makes a woman feel like she's safe in the arms of an angel."

Ryan's shoulders slumped. The big man probably couldn't dance like an angel but according to Jilly, he was a celestial when it came to sourcing rare mushrooms. I couldn't help thinking he deserved better than Tish Ramsey rubbing her infatuation in his face, and in public no less.

I glanced down at Keats to see if he agreed. Sure enough, his muzzle swivelled between them, taking their measure with his eerie blue eye. His tail was wrapped neatly around his paws but I had no doubt his white tuft would judge Tish harshly. We'd both become more judgemental since moving here, thanks to meddling with murderers. Showing that side wouldn't win me new clients, however, so I summoned my best innkeeper smile. Ryan was well connected with people who cared about and could afford saffron and stilton—the exact demographic of potential guests.

"I haven't met José," I said. "But he seems to have built a following fast. Honestly, I wouldn't have expected ballroom dance to take off here. It gives me hope for our Clover Grove Culture Revival Project."

"Ballroom dancing is culture?" Ryan asked, raising heavy eyebrows.

"Of course it is, silly," Tish said. "Maybe you should try it sometime."

The eyebrows came down fast. "I'd rather be tackled hard right before the goal line," he said.

"Oh, Ryan," I said. "I feel you, I really do, but maybe we should open our minds and give ballroom dancing a chance."

"Darling!" The voice in the general region of my armpit was melodious. "You have no idea how delighted I am to hear you say that."

Dahlia Galloway never used to sound melodious. I remembered her as shrill and harsh in my childhood. Maybe she'd taken voice lessons on the sly, along with ballroom dancing.

"I was joking, Mom," I said quickly. "I'd rather be spit on by a vicious llama than—"

Jilly gave my arm a sharp pinch as José joined us. He was as short and slight as he'd appeared from a distance and in close proximity to Ryan, looked as delicate as a doll. If there was such a thing as ballroom dancing man dolls, which I doubted.

"What Ivy *meant* to say is that we're excited about any new cultural pursuit in this town," Jilly said, releasing me and offering her hand to José. "We're opening the doors of the inn to host information sessions."

Mom's face lit up and she clapped her hands. "Oh, how wonderful. Because José has the opportunity of a lifetime for you."

CHAPTER FOUR

I folded my arms over the fence of the camelid pasture, refusing to look at Mom. "I fail to see how this is the opportunity of a lifetime for me."

"Oh darling, where's your sense of adventure?" There was no melody in her voice for me this afternoon. In her words, I'd been a "stick in the mud" and "joy thief" since she talked me into this. Or more specifically, talked Jilly into it, since it was my friend who'd twisted my arm to say yes. "Life is so much more fun when you stop judging and start dancing."

"Tomorrow I'll stop judging," I said. "Today I'm telling you this is stupid."

"Don't you dare call José stupid." Her tone was harsh, just like the old days. Maybe this man was dancing his way to the top of her rotation. "He's a brilliant, talented man and this is a fabulous idea."

I turned my back on the spectacle taking shape to our left and stared at her. She was barely five feet tall and I had to step back to look that far down. "I wasn't calling José stupid. I only just met the man. But the idea is stupid. I'm entitled to my opinion, especially when it affects my livestock."

"Open your mind," Mom said. "You used to be the visionary among my children. What happened?"

"You know what I've been through. No need to relive it."

"Don't let your experience make you bitter, darling. It's not attractive. Chief Harper needs a lighthearted woman to distract him from the ugliness of life."

I glared at her. "Chief Harper needs someone who sees both sides—the ugliness and the beauty. Because that's what *he* sees every day. Regardless, I'm missing how this performance makes sense."

"Not everything needs to make sense. Sometimes it's enough to bring light and love into the world."

My glare turned into a stunned stare. "Who are you and what have you done with Dahlia Galloway? There is no way my cynical mother would burble about bringing light and love into the world. *My* Dahlia got burned by love, remember? She keeps her distance from the flame now."

She gave an exasperated sigh. "I'm leaving the past in the past where it belongs, and you should too. I'm healing, Ivy."

"And José is the miracle cure?"

"Dancing is the miracle cure." Finally she smiled. "José is just a man—no better or worse than many in my rotation. But he's brought dance into my life. And in case you didn't notice... I'm good at it. You know how long it's taken to discover my talents, Ivy. I thought you'd want me to enjoy them."

That took me down a notch. When I refreshed Mom's résumé time after time, I always queried her on her interests and passions. The only one she ever acknowledged was redesigning clothing from secondhand stores. It was truly a gift and had allowed her to create a signature style on a shoestring budget. The cherry red dress she was wearing had a stretchy bodice from one dress and a full satin skirt from another. It was a departure from her usual look, but I knew a lot of skill had gone into creating her newest ice dancing costume.

"I do want you to enjoy your new passions," I said. "I've proven that by investing in your salon. But I don't have to like it when your passions stress out my animals."

She cast her eye over at the two llamas huddled in the corner with their donkey bodyguards. "Those llamas are grumps. They should try dancing like the alpaca. Alvina adores José. Look at her flirting."

"Alvina is flirting with Asher. He keeps her calm and centered, which is why I insisted he be here for your little stunt."

"You mean, this major marketing endeavor that will bring worldwide attention to your farm."

"Big promises. I'm not holding my breath."

I turned as a lime green van pulled into the parking area. It belonged to Bridget Linsmore, who was part of a Dorset Hills dog rescue group known as the Rescue Mafia. They'd all been close friends with Hannah Pemberton but rarely appeared on Runaway Farm now because of the frequent police presence. In fact, they only agreed to come today because I promised Kellan wouldn't be here. Asher was far less likely to throw their lawbreaking past in their faces. He was incapable of holding onto negativity for long.

"How nice that your vigilante friends could come," Mom said, brightening. "I've been so anxious to meet them. They sound like strong, interesting women."

My hackles settled slightly. Despite being a flirt and a gadabout, Mom truly did admire strong, interesting women like Jilly, and I daresay, me. But she'd never meet another crew quite like the one spilling out of the green van now. Cori Hogan, the co-leader of the Mafia alongside Bridget, was already stage directing everyone with her trademark black gloves with orange middle fingers.

"They are strong. And fearless," I said. "That's why I wanted them here to protect my animals." I pointed to a pretty woman with curly red hair whose hands were as busy directing as Cori's. "Evie Springdale filmed here all the time in Hannah's day and Alvina is comfortable with her."

I'd only agreed to let José shoot his promotional video after he agreed to my conditions: that he use my crew, follow my rules and close the event to his groupies.

"You pamper these creatures like they're delicate divas," Mom said. "They're animals, Ivy."

"They're family," I corrected. "Just like Keats and Percy and Jilly."

She turned away from the Mafia to glare at me. "I'm family. Your sisters and brother are family."

"Hmmm." I turned back to make sure José wasn't getting too close to Alvina. Asher had taken a lieu day to play human shield, further cementing his hold on the position of Mom's favorite.

"Don't you 'hmmm' me, young lady. We're higher on the pecking order than your menagerie. Besides, you're benefiting from this event, and don't forget it."

I sighed. As much as I wanted to dispute that claim, I'd fallen for the perfect bribe. José had promised that if I allowed him to make a video dancing with Alvina, he'd bring his former dance troupe to stay at the inn for two days. He needed backup, they needed accommodation, and I needed business. Jilly was inside now making sure we were ready to receive our guests.

"Let's just get this over with," I said, reaching for Keats' ears and finding empty space. He rarely left my side but with all the commotion, he was worried about the livestock. Still, he took a moment from his rounds to greet Cori Hogan with a play pose. When the master trainer was around, he always paid his respects.

"Turn that notion around, darling," Mom said. "Let's savor every moment of this gorgeous day. What a rare and exciting opportunity. I bet HR was never like this."

It was a gorgeous day, with the bright blue skies of fall and a deceptive hint of warmth in the air. Most of the brilliant leaves had fallen but from a distance there was still color in the hills. It would make a pretty backdrop to the video, however incongruous it seemed to me.

Another van pulled up and a group of people plugged the doorway, all trying to be first to get out. I shook my head and laughed. "Actually, HR was often like this, Mom. Strong personalities competing for attention."

She shrugged and pulled a cherry red pashmina out of the bag at her feet. Everything matched perfectly, from her lipstick to her fingernails to her satin pumps.

"Ivy, just for one second can you suspend your disbelief and have fun? You're my brightest star in so many ways but you were never fun."

There was a good reason for that. As the last of six in a family that struggled for every meal, my role was to be the good girl—the one who kept her head down and won a full ride to college. Like Keats, I'd never really learned to play. That was changing now, but our idea of fun would never align with Mom's.

"Ivy, help please." I turned to see José striking a dramatic pose on the makeshift stage outside the camelid pasture. "I can't get your llama to dance."

"Try calling her an alpaca, José," I called, as Alvina literally turned her back on him. "See where that gets you."

"Ivy, go help," Mom said. "Before the crowd arrives."

"What crowd?" My eyebrows shot up. "I specifically said no crowds. You and José promised."

"It's hardly a crowd," she said as vehicles started streaming up the lane toward us. "Just a few devoted fans. You can't have a video without fans."

Tish Ramsey, Mabel Halliday and Teri Mason soon gathered beside the makeshift stage along with many women I'd seen around town but didn't know. Somehow they'd managed to bribe or coerce their husbands and partners to come along, and the guys gathered over by the big red tractor, no doubt to replenish their testosterone.

"I can't believe you got roped into this," I said to Simon as he strolled past holding hands with Anne.

He gave me an impish grin. "It's called networking, Ivy. Everyone here has animals to feed, right?"

"We could learn a thing or two from him," Jilly said, joining me. She craned around at the crowd. "Where's Edna? It's not like her to miss something like this."

Our nosy neighbor would normally be the first to arrive and last to leave. "Prepper convention in Brenton," I said. Edna's mission in life now was to be ready for disaster, and that took precedence over more trivial pursuits, no matter how entertaining they might be.

"What a shame," Jilly whispered. "I know she'd enjoy mocking our guests." She stared at the dancers and shook her head. "And there's so much material. Or rather, so little."

The women's outfits were very skimpy indeed for November, but the show must go on.

"Ivy!" The shout came from Asher this time so I hurried over.

Cori was advancing on José, orange fingers flashing. "Don't ever—ever!—slap an animal again," she said. "Here on this farm or anywhere else. If you do, I will know." The orange fingers moved to her eyes. "I have eyes everywhere."

"I was just trying to make her go," José said. "She's supposed to be lively. Fun. I need that for my video."

Maybe it was my imagination but it seemed like his Spanish accent disappeared entirely when confronted by Cori Hogan's rage.

"Let's get this straight," Cori said. "I'm Alvina's agent. You speak to her through me. Got it? Otherwise, I'm throwing you to the thugs over there." She gestured to the two llamas and three donkeys. "How do you think that'll go?"

"Yes, Miss Hogan," José said. "We'll shoot on your cue."

She nodded. "That's better. As for you, Officer Smiley..." She turned on my brother. "Less teeth and more action. Alvina needs movement to activate. Flap those arms. Pump those legs. Sing if necessary."

"Sing?" Asher sounded nervous now.

"She likes Frankie Valli and the Four Seasons," Cori said. "Greatest Hits always do the trick."

"He can't sing during my performance," José said.

"I can't sing at all," Asher said. "It's not my forte."

Cori's gesticulating gloves showed her exasperation. "Like I said, I'm Alvina's agent. I know what she likes. I suggest you stop talking and start singing." She gestured for Keats to herd José to the dance floor. "Stay ten feet away from my client, Sir Dancealot. For your own safety. Because that's how far she can spit her regurgitated stomach juice."

The crowd promptly backed away from the fence and I sighed in relief that the production was now in Cori's capable gloves.

"Good," she said. "Get that music thumping because it

puts my client in the right mood. Oh, and by the way...? She spits on command and her aim is impeccable."

"Is all that true?" Mom asked, as I pushed her toward the dance floor.

"Hey, Mama Galloway," Cori called. "It's showtime. Let's see some hustle."

"I don't think I like her," Mom muttered, clinging to my side.

"No free passes for relatives," Cori called. "Alvina's an equal opportunity spitter. Chop chop, Mama G."

"Hurry," I said, grinning. "You were right, Mama G. This really is fun, and exactly what I needed."

She threw her shoulders back and strutted over, no doubt glad her heels gave her about an inch on Cori.

"Officer Smiley," Cori called. "Hit it."

Asher's face flamed brighter than the last of the fall leaves as he started singing. "Sherry," he quavered. "Sherry baby." Alvina stepped up to the fence, ears forward. The sign of her trust in him under pressure was enough to make my brother forget about the men by the tractor and launch into a falsetto that instantly made Alvina's toes tap.

Cori offered a rare smile, clapped her gloves, and then gestured for José to get moving. When he stalled, she took a little sheepdog lunge that made him hop onto the stage with a dramatic flourish of arms and legs, and the performance truly began.

CHAPTER FIVE

I t was all over in about three hours, but it felt like more. Alvina never did agree to dance with José, but with Asher dancing and singing as hard as he could, the alpaca performed beautifully. No one got hit with fetid green slime, so I considered that a huge win.

Evie showed her director chops by finding a setup that allowed Asher to be out of camera range while keeping José, Mom and his dance troupe front and center. Using a second camera, Bridget shot from different angles that could be edited in to create a seamless piece later.

It was impossible for me to like José knowing he'd slapped sweet Alvina, but I couldn't deny he'd adapted like a pro and performed well in unique circumstances. Two large speakers blasted the same music we'd heard at the studio three nights ago, drowning out Asher's singing. José took my mother out for the first spin on the small stage and she did very well, looking as radiant as I'd ever seen her. I couldn't help thinking about Tish Ramsey saying that it felt like being in the arms of an angel. After their last elaborate dip, he led her off the dance floor and offered his hand to a lady about

Mom's age and equally well preserved. Indeed, all the women from his troupe were slim, fit and dressed like figure skaters. Skin-toned netting kept their skimpy dresses in place, whereas my parka was zipped to the chin. They weren't just a dance troupe but soldiers in service of their art.

Mom wrapped herself in her pashmina and didn't resist when Jilly draped a puffy down coat around her shoulders. I knew then that Mom was demoralized by the proficiency of the other women. With every number, she seemed to shrink until she looked like a toddler in a snowsuit.

There was a reason José had elected to dance with Mom first. If she'd gone last, all of her confidence would have leaked into the cold, hard earth.

"Mom," I said. "These people are pros. They've obviously been dancing for years."

The hand she waved curved into a claw. "Don't pity me, Ivy. You know I hate that."

"I do know. And *you* know I hate cajoling you. That's why it pains me a little to tell you that the women at the recital the other night were quite jealous of your skills. They said you're a natural."

She waved the cold claw again. "They're probably saying José gives me private lessons. I know how women think."

I was guilty of thinking the same thing, unfortunately. "It doesn't matter what they think. José has only been in town a month and unless you've had previous training I don't know about, you truly are a natural."

Standing a little taller, she put one red pump forward and struck a pose. "I always loved dancing. In fact, your father and I met at a—" She stopped abruptly. "Never mind."

José did one last number with two other couples and everyone, including Cori Hogan and even Keats, stood still to watch. Their grace and skill were utterly mesmerizing. It might very well look striking against the backdrop of the farm and the hills, but Alvina's antics inside the pasture—the hopping, bucking and mad dashes—simply didn't jive. I never claimed to have an artistic aesthetic, but I was quite sure about that.

All the performers left the dance floor and gathered around Mom, Jilly and me. Once Keats felt he could stand down on livestock supervision, he moved to my side. His muzzle lifted as he did an assessment of the crowd and nothing seemed terribly amiss. After a few moments, he shifted to position himself squarely in front of Mom. When José tried to get around him, the dog kept shifting and a less graceful man might have stumbled.

"Your dog is very protective of Dahlia," José said, smiling at me. "It's adorable."

His accent was back now that Cori's attention was elsewhere.

"Keats *is* adorable," I agreed. "Mom's his favorite, next to Jilly."

Jilly stepped forward now. "You must come inside right away. Once you cool down, you'll catch a chill. There's a roaring fire and hot cider."

As we filed to the house, I noticed that Bridget, Cori and Evie had already packed up the van and were ready to leave. Cori flashed me a black thumbs-up and mouthed, "Good luck."

I doubted I'd need it. Not this time. These guests seemed warm, friendly and decidedly more animated than any we'd welcomed before. There was laughter and teasing, and one of the men—tall, bald and surprisingly supple—lifted and spun a woman on the path. She very nearly clipped my mother in the chin with her stiletto, but Keats moved Mom out of harm's way and delivered her to me.

"That was deliberate," I whispered. "She tried to kick you."

"Don't be silly, darling. We haven't even met."

"Well, I know it and Keats knows it, so watch out for stray stilettos."

"You suspect trouble everywhere," Mom said.

"That's because there is trouble everywhere."

"Only here on this farm."

"Our last bout of trouble was at your salon," I reminded her.

Jilly held the door open for us as we entered the house last. "Will you two stop bickering and remember you're co-hosts?"

That made my eyes widen. "Co-hosts?"

"Well of course, darling." Mom's voice was melodious again. "I don't consider myself a guest, even though I'm spending my first night under your roof. I'm sharing hosting duties with you because I know these people best."

"You just said you don't know them at all," I said. "Which is it?"

"I know José quite well, obviously, and since these are his long-time friends, I suppose we're hosting as a couple. More or less."

I closed my eyes briefly, knowing exactly how this was going to go. Mom would swan about lording this beautiful home over the people who had better dance moves. Her ego needed its own guest room.

Once we'd gathered around the big fireplace, José slipped a possessive arm over Mom's shoulders and introduced her to his friends. They had all driven hours to be here and seemed to hang on José's every gesture. Even the men.

"You have a beautiful home, Ivy," said Collin Morgan, the bald man, as he shook my hand a little too hard. "And it was wonderful to dance with the master again. Well worth the drive from Millbrook."

"So wonderful," said Arlene, the woman who'd nearly kicked Mom. Her platinum hair didn't match her bun, but her blue dress was the exact shade of her sharp eyes. At least what there was of the scant fabric. "Our loss in Everly Falls was definitely Clover Grove's gain."

Stacia, whose hair was coiled in a coronet, murmured agreement as she offered her fingertips. "There's never been another like José in Smithfield, either."

"Or Cedar Ridge," said Maeve, the remaining woman. She, too, had a twist of gray hair and a wisp of silver fabric covering her lithe body. I could only hope to be as fit as these people when I reached middle age, but farm work made me strong, not sinuous.

The last man, James, had plenty of gray hair and a normal handshake. "I had the shortest drive, from Brenton, but I'm happy to be staying. It's good of you and Jilly to have us on short notice." Mom cleared her throat conspicuously and he added, "You too, of course, Dahlia. How wonderful that you and José hit it off so quickly. It's not easy to find the right dance partner."

The voices of all three women overlapped as they agreed.

"I haven't danced at all since José left," Maeve said. "The men dropped out of our club and I can't even remember the last time there was a proper dance outside the big cities."

"Same here," Stacia said. "Collin and I meet up sometimes at a studio in Smithfield but it gets expensive to rent space. And a big part of the appeal is being with a crowd. It's such a magical feeling when everyone is moving in unison."

Jilly had gone into the kitchen and now returned carrying a tray of pretty antique teacups filled with steaming cider. People sipped in silence for a moment, and then

Arlene said, "That was simply wonderful... dancing under blue skies. I hope we can repeat it tomorrow without the gloved tyrant."

"Lovely idea," Mom said, flicking her eyes at me.

"It's calling for rain, I'm afraid," I said. There was no way I'd put my animals through the strain of loud music and spinning bodies again. As Charlie, my farm manager, always said, "Calm livestock, calm life."

Stacia flung out her arm. "This room is a little small but it'll do in a pinch. We'll dance after dinner."

"The floors," Jilly muttered beside me. "The heels."

"Perfect," said Mom, our co-host, letting José spin her. "How fun."

"You really must share José, though," Stacia said. "No offense to Collin and James, but few have José's proficiency."

"Of course," Mom said, with a magnanimous smile. "I'd love to dance with James and Collin, too. We haven't been able to entice any men to our club here in Clover Grove, I'm afraid. But we're hoping this video will change that. Our goal is to make ballroom dancing seem fun and accessible."

"Yes, well," Arlene said, with a chilly smile. "The camel is certainly a common touch."

"Alpaca," I said. "We don't have a camel. Yet."

"Ever," Jilly said. "Honestly, Ivy, don't even put that out in the universe. Whenever you do that, the animal always arrives."

"There are worse things than a camel," I said, grinning. "Like an ostrich."

Her blonde eyebrows shot up. "Oh my gosh. If you get a giant bird I'm going to fly, too."

"Ostriches don't fly," I said. "But they can run like the wind, I hear."

"Dahlia?" Jilly said, turning to my mom for support.

I followed her eyes and saw Mom and José gazing at each other in silence. They were having "a moment" right there in the middle of a crowd. She was carrying a torch for the alpaca slapper.

Before I could interrupt that moment, Arlene did it for me. "José," she said, a little louder than necessary. "Are you really settling down in this backwater town?"

I'd driven through Everly Falls and it wasn't exactly a thriving metropolis. In fact, it had none of Clover Grove's quaint charm.

"Please tell me you're coming back through Cedar Ridge," Maeve said.

"And Smithfield," Stacia added.

Their voices were plaintive. José was obviously catnip to the ladies.

"Ladies, I'll visit from time to time, I promise," he said. His features were nice, I grudgingly admitted, particularly his jawline and his smile. I would imagine his eyes were riveting if you didn't know he slapped animals.

"How did you two meet?" Maeve asked. "In class?"

Mom shook her head, giggling. "José came into my salon for a classic barbershop shave and left with a new student."

"Girlfriend," he corrected, seemingly unaware of the wilting of netting all around him. He took her hand again, spun and dipped till Mom's hair dusted the soon to be pocked hardwood.

"Oh my," Mom said, once she was upright. "It's all been dizzying."

"I like the town and the studio is perfection," José said. "If I can attract enough clients, I will most certainly stay."

His arm tightened around Mom's shoulders and I expected her to ease out from under it. She'd been alone too long to enjoy being squeezed that hard. I knew she felt trapped in a hug because I'd felt the same way... until Kellan.

Instead, Mom actually leaned into José, offered the room a beatific smile, and said, "I have no doubt we'll attract a crowd in no time."

We? Was she a "we" now? Earlier she'd said José was just a regular guy in her rotation. She was probably just lording it over the competition. At least I hoped so.

"We have a bigger plan, too," José picked up. "Every couple of months we'll hold weekend events so that you can all come and dance your hearts out in Clover Grove." He gestured with his free hand. "We'll make Runaway Farm our headquarters."

"Wonderful," Jilly said, before whispering to me, "We can resurface the hardwood."

Mom glanced at me and her expression seemed triumphant. I supposed it wouldn't kill me to toss her a smile if she was going to bring me regular business, but I wasn't thrilled about any of it. I couldn't be when Keats was parked on her pumps like he had reason to protect her.

"Let me show you to your rooms so you can get settled before dinner," I said. "Jilly's prepared a grand fall feast."

"Yes, let's get changed," Stacia said. "It really is quite chilly."

James and Collin looked at each other and shrugged. They were both in fitted white shirts and black slacks, just like José.

"We'll start moving out the furniture," James said.

Jilly fluttered around them like an anxious hen. "Be careful," she said. "Don't hurt your backs."

"Glad you signed waivers," I joked as I led everyone else out of the room and up the wide oak staircase to the guest wing.

"Ivy," Mom said. "No one appreciates your humor. Doesn't that bother you?"

"Not as much as you wish it would." I flung open the door to the first room and gave her a gentle shove inside. There were only two rooms in the inn with single beds. Mom was assigned to one, and José the other.

If they wanted to dance, they could do it in the dismantled family room with Keats as chaperone. I wouldn't need to ask him twice. He walked into Mom's room and flicked the door shut with one white paw.

CHAPTER SIX

My head was pounding when I woke the next morning and at first I thought the salsa music was still playing. The party had started by eight and gone on long past two a.m. I'd only been able to sleep by turning on the air conditioning unit in my room to block the noise. That meant wearing a parka, toque and mittens to bed to stand the cold. Keats, who never shared the bed because he liked to pace and listen for incursions, had finally curled up in a tight ball with Percy at my side for warmth. When I did finally drift off, it was into a dream where the three of us went winter camping and were sound asleep when a polar bear attacked.

I sat up and tried to shake off the lingering horror. "Boys, we slept through a bear attack in my dream. Can you believe it?"

Keats leapt away from Percy as if embarrassed to be caught snuggling with his frenemy. He shook himself all over and then went to the window, stood on his hind legs like a circus dog and whined.

I glanced at the clock and swung my legs over the side of the bed. "You're right, buddy. We'd better get down to the henhouse and gather the eggs before Jilly wants to start breakfast. She's doing an elaborate frittata that calls for dozens."

Percy moved into the spot I'd vacated and licked his chest before curling into a ball again. Although the cat didn't like to miss anything, he was slower to get going on cold mornings. There were blooms of frost on the glass that would have warned me to put on my warmest clothes, had I not already been wearing them.

"On the bright side, I don't need to get dressed," I said, trying to shove strands of staticky hair under the toque. The wool mittens only made matters worse. "Also on the bright side, the guests will likely sleep late. They'll be worn out and hung over."

The female guests had come down to dinner wearing different yet equally skimpy ballroom dance dresses. Mom didn't get the style memo, so she was overdressed in a red knit dress that wouldn't cut it on an ice rink. Her lips puckered in a pout that didn't ease until José twirled her through the empty family room and made sure her faux alligator pumps were the first to damage the shiny hardwood.

Jilly tried to hide her own pout as the guests mowed through dinner like woodchippers. The meal she'd spent hours planning and preparing wasn't savored or even noticed. It was mere fuel for the main event, which was the dance to follow. They waved away dessert, but accepted champagne. Mom and José whirled through a foxtrot, the mambo, and other dances I didn't know, before allowing the others to join. After that, the floor was never empty. They'd step in and out to replenish fluids with so much wine that Jilly began to worry we'd go dry.

Mom was never a big drinker and had stuck with soda, perhaps worried she'd be sidelined or even injured by the guests. Seeing she was too jittery to co-host in any true sense of the word, I finally called my sisters one by one to help babysit so that Jilly and I could grab enough shuteye to function today. Poppy was last on my list because she was least likely to be available and most likely to join the party instead of helping. Desperate times called for desperate measures however, and when she came through, I realized she was actually the best sister for the job. Poppy was the most capable of keeping Mom's ego in check, and their sharp verbal barbs clashed against the armor they shared. Jilly and I finally retreated upstairs with Poppy circling the floor like a matron at a school dance. She had a hiking pole under her arm and told me she wasn't afraid to use it.

"Keats, I'm worried," I whispered, opening the bedroom door. Every door was closed and all was silent. "That bear attack wasn't just a dream. It felt like an omen."

The dog looked up at me with his eerie blue eye glowing in the dim light. He mumbled something affirmative and nudged my hand to let him go down the stairs first.

He stopped on the landing and we looked over the bannister. The long leather couch was taking up most of the hall, having been relocated from the family room. On one end, Poppy was curled up sound asleep. At the other, Mom sat with her head back and faded red lips hanging open. A gentle snore filled the air. There was no one else in sight, so I assumed everyone had made it to bed unscathed.

I signalled for Keats to lead me past them to the kitchen, where I tucked my flannel pajamas into my work boots and stepped out the back door.

Sucking in a deep, frosty breath, I let it out slowly as we walked around the house. It was still dark and would be for a good hour. That's what I hated more than the cold and we had a long way to go before the days started getting longer again. In the city, I'd barely noticed the seasons pass... the years pass... the decade pass.

That realization gave me the mental slap I needed. I wanted to experience my days fully now, and that meant embracing the seasons. It meant being grateful for what I had, which was so much more than I ever imagined.

"It's going to be an interesting day, Keats," I said, picking up the pace. "Mom's going to have a crick in her neck from sleeping in that position, but I bet she'll still try to dance it off later. At least Poppy kept her word. I wondered if the place would be trashed."

Keats mumbled something back, but it wasn't our usual banter. He had business on his mind. The dog didn't like getting a late start. Restless animals were reckless animals, and it made his work harder.

There was a sudden bright blur as a fluffy comet cut Keats off in a blatant invitation to play. Percy had caught up and somehow squeezed past me on the way out. Normally Keats would indulge the cat with a chase just to warm up for the day. Today he dodged Percy easily and started trotting. Instead of trying again, Percy fell in step with the dog. Both of their tails—usually happy flags in the morning—were lower than half-mast.

"You're worrying me, boys," I said. "Where's the joy?"

Collecting eggs was my easiest and most peaceful chore. The soothing clucks of more than 40 hens drowned out the incessant spinning of my thoughts. Things could—and often did—go wrong later in the day, but after one violent incident in the henhouse, it had become a bastion of calm again.

Keats and Percy stopped at the same moment and both heads swivelled. I turned, too, but didn't hear anything. My furry companions were already heading toward the sound when it finally reached my ears: a dull roar that got louder by the second.

I knew that sound and it was generally welcome... later in the day.

"Oh, come on," I said. "It's barely six. Can't a gal get a moment to herself before a busy day?"

The answer came thundering through the field, headlights piercing the darkness. The vehicle was going far too fast and the lights bounced with every rock or small hill. The driver could surely see the obstacles but seemed to relish them.

That was confirmed as the ATV circled me with a flourish, and the driver gunned the engine for dramatic effect.

"Watch the pets, will you?" I said, as Edna Evans, my octogenarian neighbor, turned off the engine and dismounted with no sign of the stiffness I felt many a morning. "If you want to drive like a maniac can you do it on your own property?"

Keats gave Edna a half-hearted swish of his tail. She wasn't a dog person and he wasn't her biggest fan, but since she'd saved our lives from a cold-hearted killer, he'd softened his stance. He stared up at her expecting a greeting. Instead, she bent to make a fuss over Percy. The cat had once belonged to the feral colony Edna had overseen, but when the opinionated marmalade switched allegiance to me she'd been a good sport about it.

"Why so cranky?" she asked, straightening. The ATV's headlights created a large bright circle and we moved into the center of it. "I thought you were a morning person."

"Late night," I said. "My guests were tripping the light fantastic and wrecking my hardwood floors."

"Oh, I heard the music," Edna said. "The entire township heard the music. I called the cops and they'd had half a dozen noise complaints. They didn't bother coming out because someone is the chief's favorite."

My face burned, but I doubted she could see it. "What's with the army fatigues? Is that going to be a regular thing now?"

"On your property, yes. There's always trouble here and it's best to dress for it."

"Sometimes you're causing the trouble here," I said. "Why does everyone remember the trouble and forget their complicity?"

She shrugged. "I was an innocent victim in the henhouse debacle. Even so, I've made up for it since."

I offered a noncommittal grunt. "Did you really call in a noise complaint on me? After all we've gone through?"

Her teeth gleamed in the darkness. They were surprisingly white for someone her age, and quite possibly dentures. "I called, but your brother and the chief were off duty. I didn't bother explaining to Betty what was going on. She's dumber than a bag of hammers but a lot more talkative."

My face flushed even more. When I'd arrived at the station weeks ago carrying an old femur under my arm, Bunhead Betty had me forcibly restrained by two officers. Worse, she'd refused to believe I was seeing Kellan. It was one of the more humiliating moments of my life, and there'd been plenty of those lately.

"Well, I'd hate for the town to run out of gossip about Runaway Farm," I said, turning back to the barn. "Thanks for throwing a few logs on the fire. Now, if you don't mind, I've got work to do."

"Hold your horses, young lady." Edna's voice boomed out and then echoed back to us from the hills. As a former nurse who'd terrorized schoolchildren during vaccinations, she didn't take kindly to being summarily dismissed. "Have you checked your phone this morning?"

"No, why?" I shook off my mitten and reached into my coat pocket. After scrolling for a second, I said, "You called half a dozen times in the middle of the night. What gives?"

"How could you sleep through that din? I had an important matter to discuss with you."

"At four o'clock, four-twenty, four-fifty and—"

She pushed down the phone with one camouflage glove. "At precisely the time I saw people wandering around out here and frequently thereafter. I thought you might worry about either your guests or your livestock. But I guess I was wrong."

I grabbed her glove as she started to pull her hand away. "What did you see?"

Edna was prone to spying on my property with binoculars and night vision goggles and that hadn't stopped since we'd become—well, "friends" was too strong a word. We were frenemies, like Keats and Percy, I supposed, keeping things lively with a mixture of ambushes and rescues.

"Oh, so *now* you're interested in what an old lady has to say." Her teeth gleamed again.

"I'm always very interested in what you have to say." I offered some teeth back and added, "About my farm. Less so about my personal life or my driving."

Her exasperated sigh created a big cloud of steam. "It's a package deal. And you're lucky to get my wisdom at a steep discount."

I put my mitten back on and spun my hand to encourage her. "You were spying on the place, and..."

"I was *surveilling* and noticed suspicious activity. I think you should relocate your sow, so I can monitor her better."

I had tried keeping Wilma inside at night but her protests

disrupted the other livestock. Since Charlie had built her an insulated house outside, she was a much happier pig.

"Keats, check on Wilma, please." I gestured to the far side of the barn. Instead, he trotted in the other direction. "Is she loose?" I followed him. "Don't tell me she's loose."

"Did he answer?" Edna said, chuckling. My communication with Keats and Percy was one of the few things guaranteed to amuse her.

I heard mumbling ahead as Keats voiced concern over something. "He answered. You're right there's a problem. But it's not about Wilma."

"You can tell all that from a grumble?"

Her voice was so close to my shoulder that I jumped. "He has a different tone for different animals. Wilma's fine. The problem is with the camelids."

"Huh." Edna sounded moderately impressed. "If the dog's right, I'll give him a little more credit."

I stopped and she ran right into me. "Edna, can you bring the ATV over and shine the lights in there? I don't trust Drama even in broad daylight."

Edna slapped her hip as she turned. "Never fear, I'm packing. And I'm not afraid of a stupid camel."

"Llama," I said, sighing. "I'm still waiting for my camel to arrive."

There was a roar behind me as she pulled the ATV around and the lights flooded the pasture. Alvina stood near the gate, her big eyes wider than ever. In the far corner, the two llamas huddled with their donkey protectors.

Midway between them a dark shape lay on the ground. At first I couldn't connect the various elements to make a whole.

"Is that what I think it is?" I whispered, when Edna rejoined me.

"Only if you think it's a man," Edna said. "Dead or alive, it's hard to say at the moment. But I'm going with the former because he looks... posed."

I glanced down at Keats and learned all I needed to know. His tail stuck out straight, his ears were back and his ruff was high.

"Oh no," I said. "Edna, it's happened again."

CHAPTER SEVEN

I started climbing the fence without even thinking. "Maybe it's okay. Maybe he's just—"

"Saving the last dance for you?" Edna said. "Because unless I'm much mistaken, that's the instructor your mom's been making a fool of herself over. That's nothing new, of course. It's been a downhill spiral since Dahlia met your father at that dance forty years ago. I was there that night, you know."

"Can we not talk about that right now?" My puffy jacket hooked on the fencepost as I tried to jump off. For a moment I dangled, with my boots thrashing wildly.

Edna reached out and brought her arm down hard in a flashy arc. The sound of fabric tearing followed the slashing movement and I landed hard. "Learned a few tricks at the survivalist convention," she said.

"Did you just slash my coat with a switchblade?" I called, as she walked over to the gate and let herself into the pasture the easy way. Once the dog and cat had followed, she clicked the gate closed behind her.

"Hunting knife," she said. "You know I like to be ready for anything."

She wasn't kidding. Not long ago, she'd hidden in a cold shack to avoid a deranged criminal. The police had since emptied her stash but she'd probably restocked elsewhere. A wise prepper had many lairs.

"That was a perfectly good coat," I said, following the white tuft of Keats' tail deeper into the pasture.

"You would have hung there all day thinking about your deadbeat dad when we have deader things to worry about right now."

"You don't know this guy's dead," I called over my shoulder as I hurried toward the body.

"I'm a nurse, remember?"

"A *school* nurse, who terrorized children with needles."

"I had a life before that, Ivy, and I saw plenty of bodies, believe you me."

By now we'd reached the prone form. Keats stood well back and lifted one white paw in a point. One of his many remarkable talents was that he'd acquired the natural traits of many breeds.

"I see it, buddy," I said. "We've got this."

I shone my phone light over Edna's shoulder as she bent down to check for a pulse. The man was face down, with one arm stretched over his head, an index finger pointing toward the alpaca. His body was bent at the waist and one leg crooked, as if he were frozen in a horizontal bow.

Edna straightened. "Dagnabit, I don't like to be right about things like this."

Actually, Edna liked to be right about everything but she did offer a gusty sigh. There was no reason to discuss the person's identity. The dark ponytail was a giveaway. José had apparently taken his final bow.

After a minute or so, Percy strolled up and began making scraping motions at José's head with his front paw.

"Stop that," I said. "It's disrespectful. This is not your litter box, Percy."

There was a snuffle beside me and I glared at Edna. She'd covered her mouth with her big glove but her shoulders shook. "Sorry," she mumbled. "Don't talk about litter boxes at a time like this, Ivy. It's disrespectful."

"How can you even think about laughing? This is tragic!"

Now she lowered her glove. "People respond to stress in strange ways. Even me."

"Well, stop it. You and Percy can go and do something useful if you can't control yourselves."

"And what might that be?" Another giggle escaped her. "Shall I put on a pot of tea?"

"Edna, enough."

She waved her glove and then slapped her leg. "I'm sorry, I can't help it. I guess when you're closer to the end of days, like me, you'll lighten up a bit. I just can't help wondering what—"

"What Kellan will say," I finished. "About there being another fatal incident at Runaway Farm."

My voice dried to a rasp and floated away as I finished the sentence. I certainly wondered what Kellan would say, too. That's why I hadn't called him despite the phone still being in my hand.

"Murder, you mean," Edna said. "Just call a spade a spade, Ivy. Going through life pretending manure doesn't stink does you no favors."

"You don't know it's murder." I rested my hand on Keats' head to tap into his strength. "José could have had a heart attack after dancing so hard last night. He's not a young man."

"Again, self-delusion," Edna said. "Look at his pose. Someone left him that way on purpose."

"Not necessarily. He was an elegant man. He probably just collapsed gracefully."

She gave me a little shove. "Smell. The. Manure. This situation stinks to high heaven."

"I refuse to believe the worst until I have no other choice," I said.

Taking the phone out of my hand, she shook off her glove, bent over and directed the beam at the back of José's head. "Notice the blood in his hair. It's my opinion as a retired nurse that someone deliberately ended José's life." She glanced up at me and her own face had a corpselike pallor in the flashlight's glow. "Or something, I suppose. Maybe it was murder by camel. Or donkey. They can be vicious, too."

Drama was feisty and might well deal a death kick, if provoked. The donkeys were also capable of defending themselves or their charges. It was their job.

I bent over for a closer look and knocked heads with Edna. "Sorry, sorry," I said, as she stood up and rubbed her temple with more "dagnabits." When she simmered down, I asked, "If he got conked in the head, why isn't there more blood?"

She shrugged. "Cold weather, possibly. Or maybe he was struck somewhere else and dropped here. Like I told you, I saw at least two people moving around. If I'm honest, I thought your mom was having a private tango."

I straightened so fast it made my back twinge. "Edna, please tell me you didn't see Mom out here tangling with José."

The catlike gleam in her eyes said she wanted to toy with me longer but she relented. "On second thought, I don't think Dahlia was tangoing with José. A strong wind could blow your mother away, and while José wasn't robust enough for my tastes, I doubt Dahlia could have pulled this off." She tilted her head and then took away what she'd given me. "Not alone, anyway. They could have ganged up on him, I suppose. There's always politics in a group like that. I heard the women were hanging off his every pirouette yesterday. The grapevine was on fire."

I closed my eyes and held my breath, my hand still on Keats' head. He gave a little whine so high-pitched it was likely only I could hear. "Okay. Okay. You're right."

"I'm right?" The words threw her off guard. She probably didn't hear them often enough. "How so?"

"Not you. Keats. He wants me to calm down and focus." I glanced at José and then turned my back on the body. "I told Kellan the other night that I was getting used to seeing things like this. But I was wrong."

"You're obviously rattled if you're blatantly communing with that dog," she said. "You know I don't hold much stock with that woo-woo business."

"Oh please. You told me to interrogate your cats when you were getting carried off by the cops a few weeks ago."

"I was disoriented and in shock. I'm not a young woman, Ivy."

There was a noise behind me and I turned. "Edna! Don't take pictures of the body. It's indecent."

"It's common sense. If we're going to figure out what happened, we need a record."

"*We're* not going to do anything. This is a job for the police."

She blew out a raspberry and moved around José, still clicking. Percy sat at the dead man's shoulder and washed his paws.

"I feel partially responsible," she said. "I saw something

going on and when I couldn't wake you I called the police. I shouldn't have let Bag of Hammers Betty deter me from my civic duty. Maybe the cops could have stopped this, or at least detained the killer. So yes, Ivy, I'll help you figure out what happened." She snapped half a dozen photos of José's black lace-up shoes. "And we need to get off on the right foot. You're always chasing a snowball downhill. I prefer a more orderly approach to my cases."

"You don't have cases," I said, trying to take my phone back.

She pressed her gloved hand against my sternum and held the phone away. After scrolling for a second with her bare hand, she pressed something.

"Hi, honey." Kellan's voice boomed out over the phone's speaker and I tried harder to grab the phone. "What's up?" he asked. "It's early."

"Hi to you, too, honeybuns," Edna said, smirking.

There was a long pause at the other end. "Who is this and why do you have Ivy's phone?"

"Oh relax, young man," Edna said, skipping away from me. "Your honey is fine. She's just afraid to tell you what happened in the camel pen last night."

"Miss Evans." Kellan sounded officious now. Coplike. "Put Ivy on the phone right now."

I called out, "It's okay, Kellan. Let Edna tell you."

Maybe if I didn't actually say the words aloud they wouldn't turn out to be true. Maybe this would turn out to be a nightmare, like the polar bear attack I'd dreamed about. Maybe I could keep my distance from another highly suspicious death.

Telling Kellan myself would make it all real instantly. There'd be that moment of shock, followed by bewilderment as he contemplated what to do about the problem here. The way things were going on the farm, he'd eventually have no choice but to put some distance between us for the sake of his career. Calamity followed me like a plague of locusts.

Clearing his throat, Kellan said, "Just spit it out, Edna."

"Call me Miss Evans," she said. "A little respect, please. Because right now I'm your only lead in this investigation."

"Investigation?" he said. "What investigation? Ivy, what's she talking about? Is she maybe..."

His voice trailed off and Edna lifted her chin. "No, I am not losing my faculties, young man, if that's what you're implying."

Her indignation gave me a window to snatch my phone back.

"Kellan," I said. "Chief Harper. You need to come over here right now. And bring the whole team."

"On my way," he said. "You're okay?"

"I'm okay. Keats and Percy are okay. José Batista... not okay."

"I'll call an ambulance." His staccato delivery told me that he was getting dressed and probably hopping around as he pulled on his pants, socks and shoes.

"I'm afraid there's nothing they can do for José."

There was a long pause with only huffing at the other end. "Oh no. Ivy..."

"Just hurry, please. Before the guests get up."

Edna saw a new opportunity to be annoying. "I'll head inside and put on some coffee while you wait out here, Ivy. Get a move on it, Kellan. You're slower than molasses in a blizzard, just like every cop this town's ever seen."

Kellan offered a few tart observations in return but Edna was already loping toward the house. She wasn't a young woman, but she sure moved like one.

CHAPTER EIGHT

I t wasn't long till I heard the sirens in the distance, but those moments standing alone with José's body truly did pass like molasses in a blizzard. Keats moaned softly and kept nudging my bare hand, which dangled at my side holding the phone. Finally he leaned his full body into me and gradually a bit of warmth crept up my legs and moved slowly toward my heart. I wanted to go over to Alvina, who looked so desolate standing by the gate. The llamas and donkeys were starting to shuffle around, either frustrated by the disturbance or hungry for breakfast. The sun had finally reached over the horizon with frail beams that weren't capable of combatting the chill. Winter had sunk its fangs into the rolling hills and snow would bite even harder soon.

Percy lifted a paw to resume his litter box ploy and I shook my head. "Don't, Percy. Just relax. Everybody relax. The worst will be over soon."

The worst was already over for poor José. I couldn't imagine who'd want him dead, if that's what had happened. He was revered by his students, male and female, and hadn't been in town long enough to acquire more enemies. "Maybe someone followed him here," I speculated aloud. "He was a rolling stone so maybe he was trying to outrun old trouble."

Keats mumbled what sounded like encouragement. The dog loved a job—any job—and a new investigation would intrigue him even more than Edna. But her fascination was different. Prurient, possibly. She'd been treated poorly by Clover Grove's citizens and had treated people poorly in return. Sometimes her motives were opaque, even to an HR expert skilled in seeing what made people tick. One thing I knew for sure was that Edna was more likely to hinder than help an investigation, should one be required. Amateur sleuthing required a light touch. I helped solve crimes mostly through casual conversation and establishing a rapport with people. That definitely wasn't Edna's strong suit. She was good in a crisis, no doubt about that, but she was about as subtle as the ATV she rode in on.

Percy circled around me and landed between my shoulder blades. There was a scrabble as he tried to get a grip on the slick, split fabric, and then he hoisted himself onto my right shoulder. His ascent usually left a trail of pinpricks in my back, but the warm fluff against my cheek was welcome. Especially when he turned on the motor, as he did now. He had a truly magnificent purr, if a little rough around the edges.

"Thanks, Percy," I said, sensing his move came from a good place. "We'll be okay. We always are, right?"

The motor got louder—so loud I barely heard the crunch of tires on gravel. Kellan's SUV pulled in well ahead of the rest of the team. He jumped out and ran toward me, scaling the fence with the fluid grace of an athlete. He'd played almost every sport in high school and excelled at them all, as had my brother. Unlike Asher, however, Kellan's focus had been on academics. Back then he wanted to be a doctor. I'd never asked him what had changed his mind. We were estranged in the years where each of us made the big decisions in life. But as he ran toward me now, I was grateful he'd made the choice he did.

He swept me into a hug and for a moment I relaxed just a little. "Oh, Kellan, I'm so sorry."

"No need to be sorry. Unless you did this yourself." He pulled back to stare at me. "You didn't, did you?"

"Of course not!"

He moved away, smoothing his police jacket and transforming instantly from boyfriend Kellan into Chief Harper. "I had to ask."

"You didn't, really. But fine."

The haughty twitch of my toque dislodged Percy from his perch and he sprung lightly to land on Kellan's broad shoulder. The cat turned swiftly and sat down, facing me. The visual was a parody of the pirate with the parrot on his shoulder and I couldn't stop a nervous giggle from escaping my cold lips.

"Ivy, this is no laughing matter." He tried to swipe Percy away, but the cat just stepped elegantly across his back to the other shoulder and settled again.

"I know, I know. It's just a reaction to stress." I hated to echo Edna, but it was true. "Percy, get off the chief. This is no time for games."

"Or fur," Kellan said, as the police cars pulled into the parking lot. "The fibers literally weave into the fabric of my uniforms. I pluck them out with tweezers in the evening. It's my new hobby."

Again my lips twitched. "Sorry. I'm happy to take over that job for you, Chief."

The officers surged around us. Asher pulled up the rear and gave Alvina a pat on the way by. Her posture improved immediately. By the time he reached me, his perma-smile had faded. "Where's Mom?"

"She was passed out on the couch with Poppy when I left the house earlier," I said. "But Edna went in a few minutes ago and it's just a matter of time before—"

My last words were cut off by a scream and we all turned. Mom was rushing toward us in the same dress she'd worn last night. Behind her, in various stages of dishabille, came the dance troupe. Even the men, both in striped pajamas, couldn't keep up with Mom in her heels.

"José! José!" Mom was as near hysteria as I'd ever seen her. "Ivy, tell me Edna's wrong."

"I'm afraid not. It seems like José passed away out here overnight." I decided to downplay the violence to keep people calm. "Maybe he had a heart attack after all that dancing."

Mom flung open the gate and ran past Alvina. Keats went over to meet her and escort her to my side. "That's impossible," she said. "José was a superb athlete."

"Heart attacks don't play fair," I said. "Keats, can you shut the gate, please. I don't need to be chasing animals on top of everything else."

The dog circled around the rest of the guests and pushed the gate closed. He waited there till Jilly, Edna and Poppy pulled up the rear, and repeated the move once everyone was inside. Then he positioned himself to keep watch on Drama Llama and his shifty colleagues.

Some of the officers had crowded around José, muttering to each other as they crouched to study the body. Kellan stood like a statue with Percy still perched on one shoulder.

"Chief Harper," Mom said. "Why are you just standing around? This is no time to be playing with the animals."

His lips pressed together in a thin line and he turned his

eyes on me. I realized he didn't want to risk hurting the cat by flinging him off.

"Percy, get down," I said. "Let the chief do his job."

The cat leapt across to my shoulder again and I muffled a little scream with my mitten. He was barely heavier than a breeze, but the claws were always a shock on landing.

Keats took up the cause by coming over to make little lunges at Kellan's legs. It was as good as saying, "Do something."

Nudging the dog aside, Kellan said, "I *am* doing something, thank you very much, Keats. Have you noticed my fleet of investigators?"

When he realized he'd answered the dog aloud, and in front of his team, a flush reddened his cheeks. I felt for him but at the same time I was secretly pleased that Kellan understood my genius dog.

"Keats, can you check on Drama?" I said. "He's starting to get fidgety over there. We'll need to move the herd out so that the police can do their thing without getting trampled or bitten."

"Is that what happened?" Stacia, the striking brunette dancer, was the first to speak up. She was clutching a red silk robe over something skimpy and her long hair fluttered in the wind. "Did your animals trample José?"

"My animals are innocent bystanders," I said, craning to watch Keats try to guide the feisty animals around the crowd. As usual, Drama was resisting, taking little dives at the dog that weren't dissimilar to the ones Keats took at Kellan.

"Ivy," Kellan said. "I'll thank you not to speculate on what happened here. Could you please take your guests back inside?"

"I'm not going anywhere until I know what happened to José," Mom said, and the other women echoed her cry.

Kellan stared at Mom. Normally he was a match for her, especially while in uniform, but there was a fierce intensity to her gaze this morning. Her mascara and eyeliner had dripped down her face and her red lipstick smudged across her cheek in a macabre mask.

Sighing, Kellan turned and knelt among his officers to join the mumbled discussion. Then he stood and faced the crowd. "There will be an autopsy, of course, but our preliminary findings are that Mr. Batista suffered multiple stab wounds."

There was a collective scream loud enough to make both Kellan and me jump.

"Who would do something like that?" Stacia said. "Everyone loved José."

"Maybe that was the problem." Collin's voice was calm but it carried all the better for it. "Too many people loved José."

Stacia turned on Collin. "What are you saying?"

He shrugged. "Ever since I met him, women have been fighting over José. If Dahlia won, maybe that drove someone over the edge."

"Pardon me?" Mom rose to her full height and put her hands on her hips. "Won what exactly?"

Collin glanced at James and their striped shoulders rose and fell in unison.

"José was a ladies' man," James said. "Hard to pin down and proud of it. Seems you'd pulled off a miracle, Dahlia, if he was actually going to settle down here in Clover Grove."

"Maybe one of the many spurned ladies took issue with that," Collin said.

"I hope you're not including us in that vile slur," Stacia said, trying to keep her long hair out of her face. "We're long-time friends, and none of us are capable of such a thing."

"Just because you all had the opportunity doesn't mean any of you took it," James said. "There were other ladies. Lots of them."

"You had just as much opportunity," Arlene said. "And far more capability to take down a man."

Loud protests overlapped and I turned to see Edna off to one side, studying the group curiously. Meanwhile, Jilly wove her way toward me and then squeezed my mittened hand in solidarity.

Finally, Stacia's voice rang out over the din. "It might just as easily have been you, Collin. You didn't hide your disappointment when José defeated you in the statewide flamenco competition three years ago. And James had a bone to pick with José, too, from what I heard."

"There was no bone to pick," James said. "José stole my girlfriend fair and square. If he could win her, she wasn't mine in the first place."

Maeve spoke for the first time. "Collin and I were the last ones to bed at around three and there was no sign of Dahlia at the time. I assumed she was upstairs getting a private lesson with José."

"I doubt that," Stacia said. "I don't think they were serious at all. José asked to meet me privately in town today."

"Me too," Arlene said. "I know for a fact that Dahlia overheard that. She pulled José aside and they had words."

Kellan was standing with his hands shoved into the pockets of his black jacket. His eyes flicked back and forth, as if watching a riveting tennis match. Edna, Jilly, Poppy and I were doing pretty much the same thing.

"Mom," Poppy said. "Did you have words with José last night? I was barely out of sight for five seconds."

She turned on my sister. "You know I'd never let any man hold that much sway over me, Poppy Galloway. I have a very full rotation of fine gentlemen." She gestured to the barn. "There's Charlie, now. Another man I enjoy dating. José was the best dancer, that's all."

There was a murmur through the crowd and I raised my hand. "Mom. You've said enough. Chief Harper knows you didn't kill José Batista in a jealous rage." I turned to Kellan. "Don't you, Chief?"

He blinked and shook his head, processing the barrage of information. "Go inside, folks. Warm up. Have some coffee. When I'm done here, I'll speak to you one by one."

Mom spun on one heel, raised her hand and snapped, "Poppy. I'll need a ride home."

"*Everyone*," Kellan called after her. "Including you, Ms. Galloway. Go inside and stay there."

She kept walking. "I am not submitting to another inquisition, Kellan Harper. Every time I turn around, you're accusing me of murder." There was a louder murmur through the crowd as people picked up on Mom's illustrious past. "So if Poppy won't drive me home, I'll hitch a ride. I've done it before."

"Mom!" Poppy and I spoke over each other.

"Fine, I'll take Buttercup. I still have her ownership papers."

Mom's ancient yellow Volvo was now in my care—partly to keep it out of Mom's reach and partly because it was safer for me to drive than my pickup truck with its feisty standard transmission.

"But not a license," Kellan called after her. "Officer Galloway. Take your mother inside. You have my permission to use force, as required."

"That won't be necessary," I said. "Keats. Escort Mom to the house, please."

The dog left the livestock, which he'd gathered in a

corner, and raced over to Mom who turned to watch. The closer he got, the lower he got, till his white belly nearly touched the frosty grass. His eyes fixated as he tried to hypnotize her like he did the livestock, with varying degrees of success.

The ploy was a flop with Mom. Instead, she shook her finger at me. "I will not be herded like a common goat, Ivy Rose Galloway."

"Keats, you have my permission to use force, as required," I called.

The dog took his first lunge. Mom squeaked and wobbled on her heels. He'd probably given her the sharp little nip that got any critter moving, great and small. Including Kellan. I glanced at my boyfriend and found him fighting a losing battle with a grin. Finally he coughed into his glove to avoid looking unprofessional.

Keats drove Mom to the house with short arcs and occasional nips that made her hop. The squeals carried back to us on the breeze and Edna and Poppy made no effort at all to hide *their* grins.

"May I suggest the rest of you head inside before you meet the same fate?" I said, forcing a smile. "I don't know about you, but I could certainly use a coffee."

Jilly tugged on my arm and whispered, "I set up the industrial urn. That's why I was a little behind. I figured you needed coffee more than company."

"You made the right call, my friend," I said, letting her tow me out. "I'll get fuelled up and then get to work."

"Feeding the livestock?" Jilly asked, as we trudged toward the house.

My boots had never felt heavier as I squeezed her hand. "Solving a murder. Again."

CHAPTER NINE

"I'm coming," Edna said, crossing her arms and leaning against Buttercup.

"You're not coming," I said, mirroring her pose. "It's a family meeting. That means it's for family. Surprise."

"If Jillian is going, I can go."

"Jilly's family," I said. "Everyone speaks freely in front of her, and they won't if you're there, Edna. You know that."

"You underestimate my interrogation skills," Edna said. She pulled out a small plastic box, selected a tool and then tried to pick the lock on the driver's door.

"Leave Buttercup alone," I said. "And it's not an interrogation. Just a convening of my nearest and dearest."

Edna laughed. "Your nearest and dearest are out in that barn, Ivy Rose. Your family are thorns in your side."

I didn't bother to refute that. "Regardless, we *are* family and we're having a meeting. End of story."

"Fine. Don't give me a ride. I'll take my ATV."

Jilly tried to grab her arm. "You can't drive that thing across town, Edna. It's not safe."

"And you're not licensed to drive anything," I said.

"As if any cops are available to notice," Edna said. "They're all out in your pasture and Bunhead Betty is running the show at the station."

I noticed she'd dropped "Bag of Hammers" in favor of my nickname for Betty and felt a little proud.

"I care about your welfare, Edna," I said. "In fact, I risked my life protecting you not so long ago."

"A favor I've already repaid." Her eyes flashed in defiance.

"True. So let's leave it at square then. Don't make me send Keats after you, too."

She sniffed. "I'd like to see him try. Unlike your mother, I'm armed and dangerous."

"You're not," Jilly said, horrified. "Edna, you can't carry a gun around."

"Jillian, I may not be licensed to drive but I am licensed to carry firearms." She gave a little chuckle. "What a world we live in."

"Do I need to describe what I'd do if you harmed my dog?" My voice was perfectly modulated, HR training at its finest, but something made Edna ease away just a little.

"No need to get testy," she said.

"Don't even joke about hurting Keats," I said. "Or Percy for that matter. I may not be licensed to carry, but I'll protect them with my life, just as they will me."

"Ladies," Jilly said. "Everyone's on edge for obvious reasons, but we're on the same team. I'd go so far as to say we're all family. Right now, we just need to disperse and get this sorted as soon as possible. Edna, I'm going with Ivy because I care about Dahlia and she knows it, so she's more likely to share information. It would be super helpful if you'd go inside and surveil the guests while we're gone."

"The chief's already inside talking to people," Edna said. "Which is why you're sneaking off to plot against him."

"I am not plotting against him," I said. "We're just... strategizing."

"In other words, plotting. May I remind you I'm invested in solving this case, too?"

I pushed off the car. "Edna, I know. And Jilly's right. While Kellan interrogates people individually, the rest will be chitchatting. Make them more coffee. Circulate. Eavesdrop." I waved one hand and flushed her away from the car. "Be nice."

Edna adjusted her glasses to enhance her stare. "You do know me, right? Nice isn't my style."

"It's a skill in your toolkit, Edna. Pull it out for a good cause."

I opened the door and let Keats into the car. There was an orange flash as Percy followed.

"Are you saying even the cat gets to go and I can't?" Edna said. I'd never seen an octogenarian pout before.

"Percy needs to stay in the car. He's not allowed inside with Daisy's ferrets. For whatever reason, he'd prefer to cool his heels in Buttercup than stay here."

Her pout turned into a sly smile. "I could take the truck. I know how to drive it, unlike you."

I slid into the car and Jilly walked around to the passenger seat.

"If you can hotwire the truck and get to Daisy's house before we're done, I'll roll out the red carpet. Deal?" I poked my head out. "Or you could just do something useful and pry information out of the guests."

She turned her camouflaged back and stomped off. "Don't think I'll always be so easily manipulated, Ivy. I wasn't born yesterday."

"If you could start by getting Mom onto the porch that would be great," I called after her. "Kellan already spoke to her and said she could come, but she's resisting family arrest. I don't want to carry her if I don't have to."

Edna's cackle floated back to us. "I'd love nothing more than to wrestle Dahlia into the car, just as I used to wrestle with your brother before vaccinating him. I still have my chops."

"That's the spirit, Edna," I called. "Go get her."

She raised her hand and it looked like she shot me the middle finger, but perhaps the stress of the day had made me paranoid.

"I WILL NOT BE MANHANDLED like a child," Mom said, as I perp-walked her up Daisy's driveway and into the house.

"It's either me or the dog," I said. "Which is it?"

She looked down at Keats, whose white-tipped tail whipped back and forth ingratiatingly. Now that he was off duty, he wanted to make amends, but Mom was as pouty as Edna, only with scarlet lips. While everyone else had filled up on coffee and gossip, Mom had done her face and hair, and put on a black dress of Jilly's that befitted a woman in mourning.

"We'll get things straightened out in no time, Dahlia," Jilly said, patting Mom's shoulder. "This is just a strategy session. To make sure we're all on the same page."

"Jillian, I'm grieving," Mom said. "I'd like to be left in peace. There's no 'strategy' required."

I kept her moving through Daisy's front hall and into the kitchen and didn't stop herding until she was parked on her favorite stool. My older sister, a clean freak, put down her spray bottle of disinfectant and peeled off her rubber gloves long enough to pour coffee into white mugs. The one she slid over to Mom was only half full. It was Daisy's latest attempt to minimize lipstick damage to her china. Mom peered into the mug, smirked, and then planted a big kiss on the rim. Game on.

Iris and Violet were already seated at the kitchen table. Poppy had followed me in her own car, having refused to ride in Buttercup's backseat due to supposed carsickness. It was more about Mom-drama-sickness, and I didn't blame her for wanting a little space.

After leaving a half-ring of lipstick on the mug, Mom spun on the stool to treat us all to a glare. "I'm not saying a thing until Asher gets here. I don't trust any of you."

"He's not coming," Poppy called as she stepped into the front hall. Her cheeks were rosy from the cold and it struck me that she was as attractive as Daisy, who was said to be the prettiest Galloway Girl. But Poppy seemed committed to downplaying her good looks with wild hair dye and thrift store punk clothing more suitable for a rebellious teen. "Kellan wouldn't give him the time off."

"Oh, he's coming," Mom said.

"You ordered him to defy the chief?" Daisy said, pulling her rubber gloves back on.

"I didn't say a thing." Mom freshened her lipstick for another assault on the mug. "He'll come because Jillian's here."

Jilly's cheeks became rosier than Poppy's. "I'm sure that's not true," she said.

There was a bang as the front door crashed open and orange fluff streaked past.

"I let the cat out of the car, Ivy," Asher called. "He asked to come in and I couldn't say no. It's cold out there."

I shook my head and grinned. "It's only been a few minutes, Ash. But I'm glad you're taking requests from my pets."

"Alvina's changed me," he said, flinging his coat on the pile on the chair and sliding in behind Jilly's seat. I had the distinct impression he wanted to protect her from our family, not realizing that Jilly's headhunting experience made her impervious to most slings and arrows. Nothing my family did shocked or upset her. The same couldn't be said for my brother. As many atrocities as he'd seen in his work, he maintained a stubbornly sweet naïveté that was shaken only by family strife.

"You didn't risk your job over this, I hope?" Daisy asked, spritzing cleanser on the already sparkling counter. "The way things are going in this family, we need an insider on the police force."

"The chief thinks he needs an insider in this family," Asher said, grinning.

"What am I?" I asked. "An outsider?"

Asher just grinned harder and brighter. "You're in a category unto yourself, sis."

"So Kellan sent you to spy on me?"

"He sent me to spy on you strategizing against him. Isn't that sort of fair?"

"He's got a point," Jilly said. The combination of their brilliant smiles was blinding. They'd make gorgeous children one day, if circumstances didn't scare her away from Clover Grove forever.

"The point is that we are on the same side, just working different angles," I said. "Kellan's going through official channels and I'm working the—"

"Dangerous, illegal channels," Asher interrupted. "Exactly why he wants a man on the inside."

"Whose side are you on?" I asked.

"Jilly's," he said, without missing a beat. "You drag her off on dangerous illegal missions with you."

"There's no dragging involved," Jilly said, patting the hand that had settled on her shoulder. "I go willingly." After a second she muttered, "Most of the time."

"You go to protect Ivy from herself," Daisy chimed in. "That's not really fair to you. Or Keats." Her head whipped around as an orange streak ran by in pursuit of a slinky rodent. "Or Percy. I hope he doesn't kill the boys' ferrets. Except I sort of hope he does." She spritzed the fridge and shrugged. "You'd need to hide the bodies, Ivy."

"My job is to expose the bodies, apparently," I said. "So let's get to business before Kellan calls his spy back to active duty."

"Where he can get valuable information in clearing Mom's name," Daisy said, reaching for Mom's mug. "Again."

Mom slapped Daisy's rubber glove away. "I'm not finished with the meager amount of caffeine you could spare a grieving woman. And there's no need to clear my name." She sat up straighter on her high stool, and nearly slid off. "I didn't threaten anyone this time. Certainly not José."

Poppy gave a slow clap. "Yay, Mom. Good on you for not threatening anyone."

"Never mind." Mom flicked dismissive fingers at Poppy over her shoulder. "You were supposed to be helping me babysit those dancing fools and when you fell asleep one of them clearly got out and murdered the master."

"Excuse me? My job was to babysit *you*, while I babysat the dancing fools," Poppy said. "You fell asleep on the job first and by the time I passed out, everyone was upstairs. I didn't want to wake you, so I just settled in where I was." She looked around at the rest of us. "I'm sure she didn't move. I'd have known."

"It's okay," I said. "I mean, it's not okay that someone murdered José at my farm, but if anyone's to blame for being asleep on the job, it's me. I should never have gone upstairs."

"That's right," Asher said.

"It's my fault, too," said Jilly, always the supportive friend. "The music was just so grating."

"It's not your fault, it's Ivy's," Mom and Asher said together.

Jilly looked at Mom and then moved Asher's hand from her shoulder. "Ivy, Keats and I are in this together."

The ferret climbed over the edge of the kitchen table and raced across in front of me. The cat followed and they skidded off the other side. Iris and Violet screamed but Jilly didn't flinch. Such intrusions were matter of course now.

"And Percy," I said. "We're the dream team."

Daisy came over, spritzed the table and applied her microfiber cloth in brisk circles. "How are we going to handle this?" she asked.

"Chief Harper is handling the murder investigation," Asher said. "We're handling Mom."

"We got the short end of that stick," Poppy said.

There was a collective snort of laughter at Mom's expense. She downed the last of her coffee and held onto her cup anyway. "I don't see what's so funny about a charming, decent man losing his life. You're all terrible. I raised terrible, heartless children."

"Oh, Mom," Daisy said. "*I* raised these terrible, heartless children. It's on me." She gave a last swish of her rag and moved to the stove. "I can live with that."

"Dahlia." Jilly's voice took on the silken note of corporate handling. "I'm so sorry about what happened. Were you really close to José? Was it one of those 'love at first sight' situations?"

Mom's eyes clouded in confusion. "Not really, although I did like him very much. José knew how to treat a lady and that's not always the case with hill country men."

"Joe," Asher said. "Joe Barker from the Bronx."

Mom swivelled quickly. "Pardon me?"

"José Batista was a fraud in name and game," my brother said. "He swindled people. That's why he was constantly on the move."

"Aha! I knew that accent was fake," I said.

My eyes were on my mother and I noticed a flush start around her neckline. She covered it with one hand as if trying to shove it down. Meanwhile her eyes darted around the room, from the sparkling fridge to the buffed countertop.

"Mom," I said. "Did José—*Joe*—ask you for money?"

She plucked at something on her black dress. Orange cat hair, probably. "He did, actually."

"Tell me you didn't give it to him," I said.

"Just a little. To get the studio on its feet."

"Mom!" The chorus of six voices included a "Dahlia" from Jilly.

"Oh, relax. It wasn't much. Only a thousand." She pretended to sip from the empty cup and muttered, "Or two."

"That was *my* money," I said.

"And mine," Daisy said.

"Mine too," the others echoed.

We'd all kicked in to keep Mom afloat as she got fired from job after job. I'd paid her rent in full for the last two years I worked in HR, but her living costs had come from the others, apparently. We never really talked about it.

"I paid him from the proceeds of the salon," Mom said, with as much dignity as she could muster.

"We're still in the hole," Iris said. "It'll be months before we can cut ourselves a wage."

"And we all invested in the salon, too," I said. "So no matter how you slice it, you let a conman charm you out of *our* money."

Mom's fingers picked faster at more hair than could possibly exist from such a short car ride with Percy and Keats. "He said he'd pay it back quickly. With interest." Her voice was as meek as I'd ever heard it. "I thought I was contributing to the revival of culture in this town. Like you wanted."

I got out of my seat and walked over. "What really happened? Did you fall hard for this guy?"

She shook her head uncertainly. "No. I kept up my rotation. In fact, I accepted more dates than ever to offset his appeal." Gripping my hand, she stared up at me. "It was his dancing, Ivy. You had to experience it to know. It felt like..."

Her voice trailed off and I filled in the blanks. "Like being safe in the arms of an angel?"

"Yes!" Her eyes brightened. "I'd never felt anything like it." Then she wilted again. "I guess I got swept away."

"Happens to the best of us," Poppy said. My rebel sister had been duped by more than her fair share of deadbeats. I supposed we'd all been affected one way or another by our father's abrupt departure. To my knowledge, Iris and Violet had barely dated, and aside from Kellan, I was pretty much off the market for 10 years myself. Only Daisy had married, and even that union had rocky periods I learned about while resolving the dogcatcher's murder.

"I feel... awful," Mom said, patting her still-flat belly. "Right here."

"It's anger over being betrayed," I said. Mom always needed help identifying her emotions. Ironically, I was usually the one to tell her how she felt despite having been totally oblivious to my own feelings for years. After rescuing Keats, however, I was frequently flooded by emotions, most of which I could name easily. "That happens to the best of us, too."

"I—I don't like it. That's why I never get too attached, you know."

Daisy leaned across the counter and grabbed Mom's hand. "You're not going to throw up, are you?" The very thought of vomit in her kitchen made her voice hoarse.

"No, Daisy," Mom said. "But if I do, I have this empty coffee mug right here to catch it."

It was good to hear the withering spark back in Mom's voice.

"Okay," I said. "So Joe was a scammer. What else do you know, brother?"

Asher shook his head. "Not much yet. Just that Joe was stabbed multiple times with a short blade a woman could use as easily as a man. It was far more than necessary to get the job done. Someone was really angry."

Mom patted her roiling stomach again and Daisy stooped to grab an empty pot from under the counter to place in front of her.

"José wasn't all bad, I'm sure of it," Mom said. "He wanted to put down roots here."

"Unlikely," Asher said. "He was already behind on rent for both the studio and his apartment. Getting women to kick in was his M.O. " Jilly touched his sleeve and he added, "Sorry, Mom. I'm afraid this guy was a loser."

"He wasn't a *loser*." Mom's voice got shrill. "He was a beautiful dancer and so charming."

Poppy rubbed her hands over her face and smudged her heavy eyeliner. "Newsflash, Mom. The best scammers have all the right moves and charm to spare."

Mom nodded slowly. "I suppose so. Your— Your father was a very good dancer and quite charming in his way."

Daisy refilled Mom's mug to the brim and said, "Sip it slowly."

After taking a mouthful, Mom stared into the murky depths of the mug. "I can't believe I got duped twice. I swore never again after your father. He was bad business."

Jilly got up and hugged Mom from behind. I knew Mom had to be in a state of deep despair to allow such a blatant display of pity.

"Look at what you got out of that bad business," Jilly said. "Six wonderful children who have your back, and some bonus family, too."

Keats leaned against Mom's leg and her hand dropped to his ears. She could accept the dog's comfort more easily than Jilly's.

"Yes," she said, gently disengaging Jilly's arm. "I had six kids, and all of them got the best of my genes, thank goodness. Especially Ivy." There was a general squawk of protest, including from me. I didn't want to consider myself a chip off Mom's block. "This never would have become such a mess if you didn't have that farm, though."

"You brought the mess to my farm, Mom, with the alpaca video that will never be aired," I said. "And now there's another murder to solve."

Mom slipped off her stool and snapped her fingers. "My coat, please. I need to lie down and recover. And you two"— her index finger jabbed the air between Asher and me —"need to sort this out. Quickly. Our family's reputation is at stake."

"Our family's reputation is mud," Poppy said, getting up, too.

"That's where you're wrong, Pops," I said. "It's manure. Dung. Guano. And like Edna Evans says, the sooner we accept the stench, the better."

CHAPTER TEN

Jilly decided to ride back to the farm with Poppy and Percy, and Mom with Asher. I waited till the police SUV pulled out of Daisy's driveway before telling everyone I had a few errands to run. They knew exactly what that meant. Keats and I were going to start poking around to see if there were clues to be found about José Batista's death. Kellan had the dance troupe covered at the inn but given what Mom had told us, there were likely other possible suspects in town.

"We don't have a moment to lose," I told Keats as we drove into town. "It's a race against gossip."

The dog's paws were on Buttercup's dashboard as he embraced our new challenge. I took it as a sign of being on the right track. If he thought the murderer was at Runaway Farm, he would probably want to be home to guard the animals. On the other hand, he might trust Kellan and Asher to keep the peace there while we sniffed for a trail to follow in town.

"We can't possibly beat the speed of the Clover Grove grapevine," I continued. "But in situations like this, it's critical to get in early before people fully shape their narrative. At this point, they don't know who's saying what and where they fit into the picture. Factions are already forming. People are deciding who's guilty and building a case against them, fairly or otherwise. It's all about redirection and obfuscation."

Keats mumbled agreement and his white paws danced on the dash in a go-go-go.

"Gotcha, buddy. But we're hitting Mandy's Country Store, first. She could point me in the right direction. There are so many suspects this time. Particularly the women from José's—Joe's—classes. Mom probably wasn't the only one he tangoed for cash."

Keats gave me a blue-eyed stare. "Okay, that was tacky, and I know you love Mom." I shook my head. "I'm still rattled and I'd better settle down. This is big. Really big. I've never heard of anything like it in the history of Clover Grove."

Main Street looked picture perfect as we passed through town. Every day it became more and more like Dorset Hills, our more popular neighbor. Better known as Dog Town, Dorset Hills had pitch perfect branding that attracted tourists from across the country. Clover Grove had once been the larger community, known for its culture as much as its agriculture. In recent decades, our town had lost its luster and half its population. Then the homesteaders jumped on low housing prices and a new sun rose. We had the chance to create something unique, but Town Council preferred to copy Dog Town's model. Perhaps in time we'd see knockoffs of Dorset Hills' signature dog statues, too. In our case, that would be huge bronze chickens since backyard coops were all the rage here. A snort of laughter escaped me at the thought and Keats turned to join in with his wide-mouthed pant.

Mandy's Country Store was nearly halfway back to Runaway Farm, but I sensed we should kick off there. Nearly everyone passed through Mandy's at some point in the week and they confided in her far more than they ever had in her grandmother, the previous owner. She was painfully shy and quiet, which made her a natural confidante. On top of that, she was a master baker and sweet treats loosened lips. I wasn't immune to the influence of sugar myself, and if I was going to stay abreast of the gossip all day, I needed more fuel than coffee.

We parked Buttercup beside the antique style sign and went inside. Mandy McCain waved from behind the cash register as I took a stool at the counter that ran the length of the front window. Normally the stools were full, but today it was just me. I couldn't help but wonder if that had something to do with what had happened at my farm.

Mandy and I had clashed when the dogcatcher was murdered and she lied about things that could have saved me a world of pain. But I knew better than most how people behaved when terrified and hurt. Human resources had taught me that before there was murder in the mix. So I'd decided to let bygones be bygones and continue to commission Mandy to provide baked goods for the inn. In a town this small, it was too much trouble to hold a grudge. That didn't stop other people. Town Hall probably had a ledger to record who hated whom about what. It was quite literally political. You couldn't get a thing done if you didn't navigate the interpersonal land mines, some of which dated as far back as our farming roots.

Keats took up his position beside my stool and mumbled a question. "Not sure where to begin, buddy," I said. "All I know is that today is going to feel a lot like log rolling. We're going to jump from one person to the next without stopping, and without thinking too much about it. The key is to capitalize on uncertainty, just like in HR. You get in fast and ask the right questions while things are still in flux. By tomorrow, people will have their stories firmed up. So get ready for a long, hard day."

The dog yipped with excitement. He lived for long, hard days.

I was perking up, too. It felt good to be doing something rather than hanging around the farm feeling like a victim.

Mandy came over and I asked about the daily lunch special, although it was just after 10 a.m. The main course was mushroom quiche, which I happened to love, and the dessert pumpkin pie, which I loved even more. As she left to collect my brunch, I grinned at Keats.

"Pie, pie and preparation. The trifecta of successful sleuthing."

Mandy circled back with a cup of coffee I hadn't ordered. I'd already had enough caffeine, and clanging nerves never helped the diligent sleuth. Worse, in the many stops I planned to make, there may not be restrooms.

I drank it anyway. There'd been precious little sleep the night before and I needed to be sharp, too. Observation was the diligent sleuth's superpower.

"How about we start with the people from the recital?" I asked Keats. "Everyone's going to be throwing shade on each other. We'll head into town and you check out the vibes."

Keats mumbled a promise to do his best. As if there were any doubt.

"You two are having quite a conversation," Mandy said, sliding a double sized slice of quiche in front of me. The upside of surviving our quarrel was that my servings were larger than anyone else's. I made a point of finishing every bite she offered, both to prove that my beefs were behind me, and to make sure the food kept coming. Between her baking and Jilly's magic in the kitchen, the eating had never been so good. Farm work and stress burned it all off.

"There's plenty to talk about," I said, not in the least embarrassed she'd caught me chatting with my dog. Mandy had plenty of quirks, too. "I'm sure you heard what happened at the farm."

She nodded. "Such a shame about José. He was utterly charming and was always trying to enlist me for his classes. Of course there's no one in town less likely to merengue than me."

"Just as well," I said, around a mouthful of delicious quiche. There were hints of tarragon and thyme, just right for this time of year. Maybe what I'd been through just made everything more savory. "José may not have been as charming as he seemed."

"Really?" The crease in her brow told me news about the scamming hadn't circulated widely yet. That would certainly help my quest. "He seemed genuine and very fond of your mother. They came in often and he was so solicitous."

I held back a shudder. "You know my mom. I'm sure she's here with other dates, too."

Mandy smiled and the crease disappeared. "I'd love to know her secret. It's hard to find good men in Clover Grove."

"Well, you're in the right place to meet them," I said. "Everyone comes through here, and once they taste your baking, they're hooked. Like me."

She pushed her flyaway blonde hair behind one ear and smiled even more. The shy girl I knew in school was transforming into a confident woman.

"How's your mom holding up?" she asked. "I sensed there was something special between them. Maybe I was wrong."

"José was at the top of her dating rotation, and she had hoped to help boost the culture movement in town with him. But she'll bounce back quickly. Too quickly, probably. All it will take is the next single man who comes into the salon for a classic barbershop shave."

Mandy laughed. "I wonder if everyone else will recover so easily. José had a bit of a cult following, from what I could tell."

"I noticed that too. At the recital, women were, well..." My voice trailed off as I chewed another mouthful of exquisite quiche.

"Falling all over him?" Mandy offered.

"Exactly. There seemed to be some competition."

She nodded. "I didn't want to say so out of respect for your mom, but he had a different lady in here every day. Sometimes twice a day."

My eyebrows shot up and the quiche lodged in my throat till I coughed. "Seriously? That popular? Who were the frontrunners, if you don't mind my asking?"

Pressing her lips together, she paused. Her business relied on keeping things quiet. But she owed me, and she knew it. All the quiche in the world couldn't make up for my almost getting killed because she withheld the truth from me —and the police.

"Tish Ramsey," she said, starting to count off on one hand. "Mabel Halliday. Teri Mason."

"Teri? I can't believe she'd fall for his so-called charms."

"I'm just saying they met here a few times and seemed pally."

I shook my head. "Who else?"

"Some of the former Bridge Club buddies."

So Joe Barker bilked senior citizens, too. I suppose that was no surprise. There was no love lost between me and the

Bridge Buddies after their atrocious behavior when they stayed at the inn. But still, scamming seniors was just the lowest of the low.

"Anyone else?" I asked, trying again with the quiche.

"Nadine Boyce. Margie Hodgson. And Dina Macintosh from the Hound and Furry." It looked like she wouldn't have enough fingers for all the ladies Joe had wooed. "Come to think of it, he brought me a lot of business."

"He'll bring you business for weeks to come as people gather and share stories about what happened."

"True. The one I feel worst about is Laurene Pedal. She's new in town and so nice. I sense she fell pretty hard for José and I'm afraid this will put her off Clover Grove entirely."

"I've heard the name but can't place her." I pushed away my empty plate and pulled over the massive slab of pumpkin pie with whipped cream.

"She's just launched the new café-bookstore called Pages and Pastries. I go in all the time, even though technically, she's my competition."

I closed my eyes blissfully over the explosion of fall flavours in the pie. "There is no competition, Mandy."

"Not with the pie, perhaps, but the book curation is top notch. Go in and see."

"We will." I glanced down at Keats, whose tail twitched an affirmative. "Are you saying Laurene was a regular, like my mom?"

"Very much so, yes." She paused for a second, and then shrugged. "I think she was taking private lessons, too. One night when I was driving home I could see into the studio windows. It was after nine and they were whirling around like they hadn't a care in the world."

I sighed as I plowed through the pie, already five bites past full. "Looks like we're going to be busy, Keats."

Mandy got up and returned with a bowl of water and a pepperoni stick. Keats wasn't a mooch, but he eagerly worked through his repertoire of tricks and brought the smiles back to our faces.

"You know I'll have to feed all of this information to Kellan when he shows up, which he always does," Mandy said, as Keats downed his treat in two bites.

I spun on the stool and hopped off. "Understood. For the moment, he's got his hands full with a frisky troupe of dancers at the farm. Including my mom."

"Drop back when you can," Mandy called as we hurried to the door. "I'll do my best to feed you first, Ivy."

I flashed her a smile that was no doubt speckled with various herbs and spices. "Thanks, Mandy. We can run all day on what you served this morning."

CHAPTER ELEVEN

I parked on the outskirts of town, partly because we had a few stores to hit on either side of Main Street, but mainly because Buttercup's unique model and color announced my whereabouts. There had been enough mayhem at the farm since I moved home that people would eventually expect me to flit about asking questions. My goal was to be the early bird with the worms of gossip.

"What do you think?" I asked Keats, who trotted briskly at my side. He didn't need to be leashed but I hooked him up in town anyway to avoid critical commentary. There was so little gossip I could control, I was willing to endure his disappointed glance. "Should we head straight to Teri's or stop at this new bookstore-café first?"

Keats didn't offer an opinion straight away. He waited till we got to Pages and Pastries and then applied both his blue eye and his nose to the door. His tail waved an affirmative.

I pushed open the door and what struck me first was the smell. I'd expected a waft of coffee and baked goods, or maybe a stuffy gust of old books, since Laurene sold used as well as new. Instead, the store smelled—well, *stunk* really—of cheese. The previous owner had tried long and hard to sell the store and now I knew why it lingered on a hot market. There was no business like cheese business.

"Hello! Welcome!" someone called from the double aisle of bookstacks. A woman came out to greet me and I recognized her instantly as the brunette who'd run past Kellan and me in tears the night of the recital. I was reasonably sure she hadn't noticed us then and now I was quite sure of it.

Whatever had bothered her then was a thing of the past, because she was smiling and her warm brown eyes had a twinkle instead of tears. She was attractive and looked to be in her early fifties, with a stylish tousled bob. I marvelled again at how many attractive middle-aged women we had in town. If it was that hard for younger women to find soulmates, it was no wonder midlifers fell for a charming man who danced like an angel. Mom imported most of her dates from beyond Clover Grove, no doubt using the laptop I'd bought her. I never asked, though. Her rotation was her business unless it impinged on my business. Technically that happened when she started dating Charlie, my farm manager, but he'd been totally professional about it. Now I had no choice but to pay attention.

"Are you Laurene?" I asked. "I'm Ivy and I've heard good things about your new café."

Nodding, she gestured to a couple of welcoming brown leather chairs at the window. "Ivy Galloway? I've heard about you, too."

I noticed she didn't say "good things." At least she didn't bother to lie.

"This is my dog, Keats. I hope it's okay that he joins me. I don't like to leave him outside unless I have to. Dogs have been stolen, or worse, set loose as a prank."

"That's terrible," Laurene said. "It's okay with me unless

someone complains." She waved around the empty café. "There's no one to notice, I'm afraid."

"Slow start up?" I asked, sinking into a chair.

"I'm afraid so. People come in but they don't stay long." She sat down opposite me. "How long do you think the stench of cheese lingers?"

I shook my head and smiled. "Wrong person to ask. I spend time every day turning my manure pile. Cheese is a big improvement over that."

She laughed. "I thought it would clear out pretty fast what with the coffee I brew all day. I offer a bottomless cup just to hold onto customers but it hasn't worked. Could I get you a cup?"

"Sure," I said, although the last thing I needed was more coffee.

I stared around while she went to collect it. The décor was pretty much perfect for a place like this, with a couple of bistro tables and hoop backed chairs, antique lace curtains in the wide front windows and big bouquets of fresh cut flowers. On the leather ottoman in front of me sat a few magazines that catered to homesteaders.

"Looking for new recipes for the inn?" Laurene asked, eyeing the magazine in my hand as she passed me a mug. "I hear you have a master chef."

"My best friend, Jilly Blackwood," I said. "I got lucky there. Not so lucky elsewhere."

"I heard about the dogcatcher. And uh... the others." She looked down at Keats, and added, "What a beautiful dog."

"He is, isn't he?" I watched closely as she reached out to pat him. He didn't like strangers taking liberties, and today he deliberately ducked to avoid her hand. His tail was at half-mast, but I didn't know if that was because he disliked Laurene or her gesture. He slipped away into the book stacks, which showed he wasn't worried about leaving me alone. "Sorry, Laurene. Keats is a working dog. Cafés aren't normally his thing. But I must say you've done a wonderful job transforming the place. It takes time to attract business in Clover Grove. People like the same faces in the same places."

She nodded. "So I'm discovering. You grew up here, I take it?"

"I did and I swore I'd never come back. But the town sinks its teeth into you and doesn't let go. You'll see."

"I underestimated how hard it would be to work my way into the community. I've tried joining clubs but unless you're canning or raising chickens, there isn't much available."

"There will be very soon," I said. "Some of us are working on a Clover Grove Culture Revival Project. Would you be interested in leading a book club?"

She brightened. "I'd love that, but no one would stick around here long enough to have a proper discussion."

"Jilly and I will host it at the inn until the smell wears off." Over her shoulder, I saw Keats come out of the book stacks and go behind the counter. He was certainly being thorough. "Mind you, we have challenges of our own right now that might put people off."

"I heard," Laurene said, picking up a magazine and ruffling the pages. "What a terrible shame about Mr. Batista. People said he was a lovely man."

Aha! She was hiding something.

"I thought you knew José," I said. Keats picked up on the shift in the atmosphere and returned to my side. "My mom said you danced with him, too."

Laurene's eyes dropped and her face flushed. Clearly she hadn't built her personal narrative—the one that made her look innocent and someone else look guilty. "I had the honor once or twice, but I didn't know him well at all. He was certainly a wonderful dancer."

"Some said it was like being in the arms of an angel," I said.

"Yes!" The word escaped before she could stop it. "He was so elegant."

"It's hard for someone like me to imagine." I stuck out my foot. "I have two left boots."

Some of the tension left her pinched face. "It was like being swept away from all the worries of life for a time. I'd never had the nerve to try ballroom dancing before but he came in here and convinced me it would change my life."

"And did it?" I rested my fingers on Keats' ears. "Change your life? I'd love to sweep all my worries away, too."

Her jaw clenched, then released, as if emotions battled for precedence. "In a way, yes. It showed me what was possible. You had to experience it to know. I'm sorry you won't have a chance, Ivy. He was quite a man and Clover Grove won't be the same without him."

She batted her brown eyes and I reached into my bag for tissues. Pulling one out of the packet, she thanked me.

"I'm sorry for your loss, Laurene. Were you and José dating?"

"Oh no." She dabbed at her eyes. "I won't say it didn't cross my mind after dancing with him, but I realized quite quickly I wasn't that special." Gesturing around the shop, she added, "I have my hands full here. It's not my time to get swept away."

She got up and walked to the counter, carrying the mug of coffee I'd barely touched. I was being dismissed.

"Maybe that time will come when your book club begins," I said, following her. "I'm sure some men will join, although they probably won't be dancers. José said he had a heck of a time attracting male students in any of the studios he'd opened. Maybe that's why he moved so often."

Laurene's eyes widened. "I didn't know that."

"So he said when he filmed a promotional video at my farm. He was looking for investors in town."

"Oh? Well, of course with starting a business I wouldn't be in any position to help."

"You didn't lend him money? I heard others did, and unfortunately they'll never get it back now."

Her eyes filled again and spilled over. "How awful for those... investors. Was your mom one of them?"

I shrugged. "Trying to get a straight answer out of that woman is nearly impossible. I'll leave that to Chief Harper to sort out. He'll interview anyone who took lessons, I suppose."

Laurene's lips sealed into a thin line before saying, "A dollar for the coffee, please."

Reaching into my purse, I offered her a twenty so that she had to make change. It gave me a minute to scan the area behind the counter. Keats had raised one white paw in a point, suggesting there was something worth my attention. Nothing looked out of place in a small store until she pulled open the drawer of the cash register. The dangling key chain caught my eye.

"What a beautiful key fob," I said, as the light glinted off what looked like a glass circle with something pink inside.

She twisted the key and pulled it out of the lock. I thought she was going to show it to me but she shoved it into her pocket instead. Then she plucked out 15 dollar bills and four dollars in coins. Turning, she waited till I opened my palm and painstakingly counted out my change.

"There you go," she said. "Money for the meter."

I laughed. "Homegirls never pay for parking. But money's money."

"Keep me posted about the book club," she called after me.

"You bet I will." Turning at the door, I called back. "You should smudge the place with sage. Good for cleansing the energy, apparently. My sister Daisy swears by it."

No need to mention that the dogcatcher had passed not long after Daisy had smudged the inn. There was no way she could have cleansed the entire farm or the field in which he'd been found.

Laurene slumped against the counter. "Tried it. Turns out sage and cheese don't play well together."

I stepped through the door and held it open so Keats could follow. "I don't believe that for a second," I called back. "I think it depends entirely on the cheese."

CHAPTER TWELVE

"Where to?" I asked Keats as we headed down Main Street again. He trotted a little ahead of me, probably to avoid getting leashed again. I let him off the hook, so to speak, as I doubted we'd be walking for long. He sat properly at the next corner and stared across the street, waiting for a green light. "Wait," I said, knowing the command was unnecessary. I was far more likely to be hit by a car for being distracted than he was. Keats was never distracted, except for the rare moments he let his guard down with Percy.

We crossed on the light and he proceeded directly to Hill Country Designs, Teri Mason's store. The white paw came up in a point, and I pushed open the door.

Teri was seated at a worktable and smiled when she saw us. "What a wonderful surprise," she called, pushing back her wheeled stool.

"But not really," I said, grinning as I walked toward her. "Good fake, though."

"It *is* a surprise to see you," she insisted. "I'm not pretending I don't know what happened—at least part of it. I just figured you'd have too much on the go to stop by and shoot the breeze." Fanning her face, she said, "Speaking of breezes, Ivy... you stink. No offence."

"None taken," I said. "I stopped by Pages and Pastries first. The place reeks of cheese and I guess it permeated my clothes." I twisted my ponytail around. "And my hair."

Teri knelt on one knee to greet Keats and there was no ducking now. When he sat for his portrait, I'd heard her chatting away to him and knew she was one of our tribe.

"And your dog," she said, rising. "Sorry, Keats. Normally you smell like sheep dung but today it's more like Stilton."

He waved his tail gaily. This dog loved filth and loathed baths. A little cheese wouldn't bother him.

"So you heard about José," I said, leaning against her biggest display case.

"The sun probably wasn't even up when my phone started buzzing. The grapevine nearly shorted from the gossip."

"I'm sorry for your loss," I said.

"My loss?" Her dark eyebrows soared up to meet her multi-colored hair.

"I know you enjoyed his class."

"I'll try anything once, but I didn't renew my package. Not my thing."

"But dancing with him was like being in the arms of an angel," I said. "Or so I hear."

Now she gave a snort of laughter. "An angel? Well, I missed my chance, I'm afraid. He never once chose me for a demo. I suppose the caftan or the striped hair put him off. Either way, I ended up paired with one of the other ladies, and it didn't feel heavenly at all. In my class, your mom or Tish Ramsey usually got to enjoy the celestial experience."

"Well, at least you've got your own angel now," I said.

"How come I didn't hear about Kevin before the recital? I thought we were friends."

"Oh, we are." Small red circles appeared on her cheeks. "I don't use that word lightly, either. It's still early days with Kevin, that's all. Didn't want to jinx it."

"He seemed nice." Keats looked up at me with the blue eye, his lie detector, and blinked. "Although we didn't get a chance to talk."

"Let's have dinner with our guys," she said. "When this José thing has died down." She closed her eyes for a second. "Poor choice of words."

"I do it all the time. When you're trying to avoid a word your mind keeps pushing it on stage. At least that's my experience. Drives Kellan crazy." I tapped my fingers on the glass, trying to figure out a subtle way to proceed. Normally my HR skills did the heavy lifting but Teri was a friend, and I didn't want to trick her into confiding in me if she didn't feel comfortable.

"What's wrong?" she asked. "I mean, besides the fact that a black cloud has returned to the farm."

I propped both elbows on the case and then dropped my face in my hands. "Don't say that."

"This will blow over just like every other cloud has. I'll be here to support you every step of the way."

Peering over my fingertips, I said, "Then do you mind if I ask you an impertinent question?"

"Not at all. Impertinent questions make life interesting."

"Were you, uh, dating José as well as Kevin?"

"Dating José?" Her sputtered laughter reassured me instantly. "Ivy, come on. No matter how hard up I was for dates—and I was, I'll admit—José Batista really isn't my type. For one thing, I'm not into older men with ponytails. And for another, I need a man who likes caftans and esoteric discussions about art. I'm very much an acquired taste."

My sigh fogged up the cool glass under my elbows. "Thank goodness."

"Why would you even think that? I showed up at the recital with a date, remember."

"I heard you met up with him sometimes, that's all. Maybe my intel was faulty."

She crossed her arms and stared at me. "Mandy McCain was not wrong. José and I had coffee a couple of times. On business."

I pushed up off the glass. "Tell me you weren't investing in his studio, Teri."

"Are you high on cheese fumes? Sleep deprived? Why would I give my hard-earned money to a virtual stranger?"

"Why are you asking so many questions without answering any?" I countered.

"Fair enough," she said. "We met on business and I normally don't share the details of my transactions. Since José has passed, I guess it's okay to say he invested in *my* business. I made some one-of-a-kind gifts for him."

Keats' tail started beating like a metronome so I followed his lead. "Gifts? Like the necklaces you made for Lloyd Boyce, the dogcatcher?"

"I take it you're speaking now as Ivy the sleuth, versus Ivy the friend."

I nodded. "José wasn't a good guy, Teri. At least, not according to what I've heard through my family grapevine. He took advantage of people."

"Ah. So you're saying he didn't get trampled by your alpaca while trying to force her to dance in the middle of the night?"

"Is that what people are saying?" Outrage distracted me from my mission. "Alvina would *never* do that."

"But the llama might, right? My money was on Drama."

"Is there a wager over which one of my animals dispatched José?" I gave an exasperated twirl worthy of Alvina herself and the tie flew out of my ponytail. "Oh man," I said, as my long hair hit my face. "It smells like Gorgonzola."

"Just calm down and quit the pirouettes," Teri said, coming around the counter. "Since when do you care what people are saying, anyway?"

"I always care what people say about my animals. And my farm. And Jilly and Kellan." I smiled. "Less so about my family."

"Well, relax as much as you can and tell me what you want to know." She looked down at Keats and took a step back when she caught the intensity of his blue eye. "Does Keats actually think I did something to José?"

I shook my head. "Look at his tail. Relaxed. Look at his ruff. Down. Look at his ears. Forward."

"But look at his eyes. Or at least the blue one. He's trying to peer into my soul."

"Buddy, stop peering into Teri's soul. She does have one, unlike some of the people we've met in Clover Grove."

"Well, what's on his mind, exactly? I'm still in the early stages of being able to commune with your genius dog."

"Maybe he's curious about the one-of-a-kind art you made for José." I gestured to the dog's tail. "Witness the white tuft, now rising. Perhaps you have useful information in clearing the farm from its current cloud of doom."

"Huh. So that's how the magic happens." She stared from Keats to me, clearly impressed. Then she tapped the glass. "See that? It's something new I've been doing. Various handmade stones encased in heavy clear polymer that looks like glass." The ones on display were tiny orange, red and yellow fall leaves that dangled from earrings and pendants. "José came by and asked if I could create a special collection, just for him."

"Leaves in earrings?" I asked.

She pulled her phone out of her pocket and scrolled until she found a photo. On a blue velvet cushion lay seven "glass" circles about an inch in diameter. Inside each one, a colored heart floated that featured an ornate initial.

"I just finished a new one." Bending, she opened a drawer and pulled out a small velvet bag. Loosening the tie, she let the polymer shape fall into her hand. The heart inside the circle was scarlet and the initial at the center was glittering gold.

"D is for Dahlia," I said. My voice sounded raspy as my throat tightened.

"Or Dina or Diane or Debbie," Teri said. "There are plenty of D names other than Dahlia."

"These were for his harem," I said. "It's sickening. Are they pendants?"

Plucking at the shiny D, she let it swing from her fingertips. "A key fob. Not so sickening, right? They were probably for his best students." She gave a little shudder. "Okay, it is a bit sickening now that I think about it. But I didn't have to think about it when I was creating them. For all I knew they could be for family back home. Wherever home was."

"It was everywhere and nowhere," I said. "He was a rolling stone who exploited people."

I took the key fob and let it swing in front of my eyes until Keats whined. Then I lowered it so he could take a sniff before handing it back. "Teri, do you know where any of these ended up?"

"Only one," she said. "The L was hanging out of the cash register at Pages and Pastries yesterday. I won't deny it made me curious. Was Laurene dating him?" She tapped her phone. "Were they all dating him?"

"No idea. José definitely had some kind of magnetic appeal, though." Tying my hair again, I said, "We'd better get going."

"You're going to hunt down every single one of these key fobs, aren't you?"

"I'm sure going to try," I said. "Can you send me the photo, please? I've already forgotten half the initials."

She nodded. "I should send it to Kellan, too. It's the right thing to do. Isn't it?"

"Definitely. It's possible that one of the recipients went mad with jealousy. Until we know more, you probably shouldn't mention these to anyone else."

My footsteps were heavy as I crossed to the door, but Keats was animated. Any adventure was a good adventure.

"How about that double date?" Teri called after me. Keats' tail dropped instantly and now that Teri spoke his language she asked, "What's with the tail? Is Keats trying to tell me something?"

"Maybe," I said. "Sometimes it's like a Magic 8 Ball. Kind of vague."

"Look who's being vague," she said, following us. "I'm going to ask him straight out."

I closed my eyes. "Teri, listen. Keats doesn't lie if he's asked directly. I think it's a matter of pride. So decide beforehand if you really want to know."

She blinked at me a few times and then sighed. "I always want to know the truth, no matter how much it hurts." Stepping back so she could take in his posture, she said, "Keats, can I ask you a question?" His tail gave a half-hearted swish.

He knew where this was going and he didn't like it one bit. "Is my boyfriend Kevin a good guy?"

The gentle drift of the white tuft toward the floor said everything. Teri's normally cheery face crumpled. The one guy who'd appreciated her quirky qualities was apparently lacking character.

"It's just one dog's opinion," I said. "And trust me, that tail said so much more when he met José. Keats was so worried for Mom. Kevin isn't a terrible guy, I'm sure of it. Maybe he's just not a pet lover. Keats is judgy about that."

Teri stooped and stared Keats right in the eyes. Normally he didn't like that at all, but now he turned his warm brown eye on her and then offered his soft ears for a pat.

"Thank you, Keats," she said. "I appreciate your looking out for me. You, my friend, are a true gentleman."

CHAPTER THIRTEEN

"I am glad we had the two pies of preparation this morning," I said, heading down the street with Keats on a leash. "Because this day has drained me and it's only two o'clock."

We crossed to the far side of the street to avoid Bloomers, where Iris was working alone. If I saw my sister there was a chance I'd blurt out what I'd learned in my rounds.

"I'm so glad he didn't give that thing to Mom. I bet it was a token for his biggest supporters, and Mom came last because she could only scrape up a couple of grand from the family coffers."

When we neared the end of the main drag, Keats picked up speed and then stopped suddenly in front of Peachtree Fine Foods. We came here often with Jilly and I normally waited outside with Keats. He wasn't permitted inside grocery stores without a song and dance about his therapy dog designation and I always felt guilty exploiting it in that situation. He was a dirty farm dog that really shouldn't be near beautiful displays of unwrapped foods.

"You know you have to wait out here," I said. "Are you sure you want me to go inside?"

I knelt beside him and gave him a one-armed hug. Each time we separated I worried it might be the last time I ever saw him, even if he were safe at home with Jilly. There was a good reason I'd worked so hard to gain the therapy dog designation before we moved here. I'd improved in so many ways but my dependence on Keats hadn't faded one bit. It probably wasn't healthy for either of us, but for the moment, it was what it was.

"It's going to be fine, right?" I said.

Keats rested one white paw on my leg and turned his brown eye on me at close range.

"Right. Breathing. In for five, out for five, just like Jilly says. I don't know how I managed to survive so long breathing without thinking about it. Was life always this complicated?"

He panted a ha-ha-ha. Of course life was always complicated. My HR job had been filled with corporate land mines that destroyed careers, including mine. Now the complications were different, that's all.

We were still hunkered together near the bike rack where I'd tied Keats' leash when the door of the store opened and Ryan and Tish stepped outside. It didn't take Keats' mystic blue eye to see they were arguing. Ryan's already ruddy face was maroon and when the door closed behind them he crossed his beefy arms and turned away from Tish. Meanwhile her pale face was splotchy and her eyes red from crying. Not just the crying of a few moments. The puffy, inflamed eyes of someone who'd been crying for hours. I knew that because I'd seen it in the mirror. Before Keats, of course. After Keats, no matter how dire life got, nothing seemed worth so many tears. Why dehydrate myself over things I could either do nothing about or do something about... with my dog?

"Ryan, it's not what you think," Tish said pleadingly.

"It's exactly what I think," he said. "You took five grand out of my account without telling me. I bounced a check to the produce guys and my payment didn't go through to the refrigeration company. That makes me look bush league. Word gets around and no one will trust me."

"I said I'm sorry. I thought I could pay it back right away. But it didn't work out."

He turned to face her. "I want to know what it was for. It was my account and you owe me an explanation."

"If you wanted me to tally up every penny you should have said so when you added me to it a few weeks ago."

"That was when you said you wanted to add some of your own savings for the wedding. You never added a cent, just made this huge withdrawal."

"I didn't know you used that account for business, too. I thought it was for our future together."

He gestured to the store. "Stores like this run close to the line, Tish. I'm always one mechanical breakdown away from going into the red. So yeah, I have to dip into my savings account. I didn't think I had to make a list of rules. Doesn't it go without saying that you let your fiancé know when you're taking his money?"

"You were all about sharing when you proposed, weren't you? Then it was all 'what's mine is yours,' and 'we'll build a future together, sweetheart.'"

She used the sleeve of her coat to chafe at her eyes—a move she'd probably regret later. Gentle patting was the way to go. Mom had taught all her girls young to avoid premature aging by treating our skin like the finest porcelain. It had worked for Iris and Violet, but Poppy, Daisy and I had played fast and loose with the rules of facial care and now I wished I had listened.

Ryan's brow had deep furrows that showed the tension any small business owner experienced, even without a murder problem. "Building a future together means we need honesty. So I need to know where my five grand went, Tish. And I need it back. Like, yesterday. Now I'm paying sky high interest on credit card debt. That won't get us a wedding anytime soon."

"If you want to call off the wedding over this, fine," Tish said.

"I didn't say that." He took a step forward to close the distance between them. As a bystander—or kneeler—I could see it was a make or break moment. Ryan loved Tish and wanted to work things out. All she had to do was come clean and he'd forgive her. "I just want to know where the money went and when you can repay it. That's not too much to ask, is it?"

"I'll pay back every cent, Ryan, I promise. But it may take a little while. You know I don't earn much working in day care. But I'll take a second job. The Berry Good Café is looking for wait staff."

Ryan's shoulders slumped. "So the money is gone? Like, really gone?"

"I don't know. I'm not sure yet." She angled away so that she didn't have to meet his eyes. "It looks like I made a bad investment but I thought it was a sure thing."

"What kind of investment?" His voice was lower now. Eerily calm.

"The kind that could have moved up our wedding date. I don't want to wait two years to get married. I'm not getting any younger."

Ryan wilted even more. "Then I'd better get the money back, hadn't I? Just tell me where to look for it."

"Just leave it to me. It's my problem and I'm dealing with it."

"It's not your problem, it's our problem. My problem, actually."

Tish began to pace back and forth on skinny stilettos even Jilly would have trouble wrangling. "I'll handle it. I'll pay you back."

Catching her hand, he gave her one last chance to earn back his trust. "Tell me. We can handle it together."

"I made a mistake and trusted someone who let me down. That's all. People get duped all the time."

A shadow passed over Ryan's face as he pieced things together. "Someone? Who, exactly?"

"A friend, or so I thought. Turns out I was wrong. You really can't trust anyone, Ryan. The world is full of scammers preying on sweet, gullible people like me."

Some of the confusion seemed to clear from his eyes and he stepped in front of her to stop the pacing. "I called you last night. Over and over. When I realized the money was gone."

"I was sleeping. Never heard the phone."

"That's why I drove over, and your car wasn't there."

"I stayed at my sister's place. You knew I was babysitting last night."

"Only your car wasn't there, either."

"Of course it was. I parked around the back because wet leaves ruin the car's finish. You told me that." She tried to move out of his path. "Let's talk more about this later. I just want to go home and freshen up before applying for work at the café. I'll need to take evening shifts. We probably won't see each other as much."

If she hoped to play on his affection, the ploy failed.

"Fine," he said. "The sooner you can repay me, the better. It's a shame I can't buy back my reputation as easily."

Resting her hands on her hips, Tish said, "I really think you're making too big a deal out of this. It's only money. We still have each other, Ryan."

"Right," he said, stepping away and reaching for the door handle.

"What's that supposed to mean?"

He turned and appraised her with what I could tell was a last look. "It just means we're different, that's all."

After the door closed behind him, Tish started to follow and then changed direction, wobbling toward me. I decided to stay where I was till she passed. But of course she looked down and her bloodshot eyes widened.

"Ivy? What are you doing down there?"

"Hugging my dog. You look like you could use a hug, too."

She shook her head. "Not from a stinky dog, thank you very much."

"He's not stinky," I said, deliberately sniffing Keats. He smelled of manure, hay and a hint of Stilton. "Okay, he is stinky. And dirty, too. But a hug's a hug on a bad day."

"You'd know, I guess." She chafed her eyes with her sleeve again. "I heard you found—found José. Trampled by your camels. I called the police about it and that's all they would tell me."

I was reasonably sure even Bunhead Betty wouldn't tell a citizen anything about a murder investigation in progress. It was just the regular gossip newsfeed.

"José wasn't trampled by my alpaca, llamas or donkeys," I said. "I don't know why he was in their pasture, but it's unfortunate he died there."

"He didn't just die, did he?" Somehow, her bloodshot eyes managed to get very sharp.

I was curious about what people were saying. "What do you mean?"

"I mean people die at Runaway Farm all the time, and not from natural causes."

"*All the time* is a bit strong, isn't it, Tish? Anyway, it sounds like you know more than I do about what happened to José. Is that what you and Ryan were really fighting about?"

"How would I know anything?"

"Because you gave José money and you don't want Ryan to know. He'd never understand that you were just helping a friend start up a business. You were trying to bring some culture to this town."

"This town needs more culture," she said. "But Ryan doesn't see it that way. You heard him at the recital. With him, it's all sports-sports-sports."

"But you thought José would pay you back with interest. And now that can't happen."

She withered me with a puffy-eyed squint. "I know about you and your ways, Ivy. People say you're a snake charmer."

"A snake charmer? That's a new one."

"You lured Lloyd Boyce's python right out of its cage to get to a treasure. By singing to it. That's what I heard."

I buried my face in Keats' fur to muffle the laughter. "That's not quite how it happened, Tish."

"You talk to snakes and you talk to animals, Ivy. Everyone knows it. You're not normal."

I raised one hand. "Guilty. But what does that have to do with José's passing?"

"José never asked me for money, Ivy. Maybe he asked your mom, though, and you wanted him out of her life. So you sang to your stupid camels till they..." Her voice trailed off. "He was a good man. You didn't know him like I did."

"All I really know is that he danced like an angel, Tish. You told me that."

"Yeah." She pulled in a breath and hiccupped. "And now he's truly an angel. But I wouldn't expect you to understand the power of dance. Look at your boots."

She made a gesture and her purse slipped down her arm and clipped me in the head. Something sharp struck my cheek and I gasped.

Keats lifted his lip a little and I felt the growl in his chest as I held him.

"It's okay, buddy," I said, rubbing my face. "Tish didn't mean to smack me with her keys. Did she?"

It was rare for Keats to show teeth in any situation other than a murderous attack.

Tish gave a twisted smile that showed her braces. "My purse has a mind of its own sometimes. Just like your camels."

As she pushed it back up to her shoulder her keys jangled. They were clipped to one of the metal rings securing the straps.

Hanging from the key ring was a green heart adorned with an ornate letter T, all encased in shiny fake glass.

CHAPTER FOURTEEN

I was so convinced Tish was José's killer that I almost didn't bother stopping by Mabel's Mutts. But I had to pass her shop anyway to get the car, and Keats wanted to go in. His tail was up, so I suspected the visit was more about the ceramic canister on the counter in the shape of a beagle that just happened to be filled with liver treats. While not a mooch, he wasn't stupid, either. With the life we led, timely meals were no guarantee.

Mabel was sitting at her worktable when we stepped inside. She looked up at me through magnifying goggles that made her blue eyes look huge. In one hand was a tiny figure of a dog and the other a slim paintbrush. Her creations were known for their exquisite attention to detail. Aside from the many she sold here, she supplied several stores in surrounding towns, especially Dorset Hills.

"Hi, Mabel," I said. "How's business?"

"Crazy," she said. "Christmas is always my busiest time but this year it's insane. I can't keep up with demand from Dorset Hills and I've stopped trying. I can only do my best."

I walked over to a table that held all of Clover Grove in

miniature, surrounded by tiny twinkle lights. Leaning in carefully, I said, "Hey! Is that Runaway Farm?"

"You tell me," she said.

A red barn that could fit in my palm sat on the outskirts of the ceramic town. There were several fenced, snowy pastures filled with sheep, goats, cows and... "Alvina! You made my alpaca!"

"I did. But it's Alvina at rest, because molds for dancing alpacas were hard to come by."

"That's because she's one of a kind," I said. "You totally know I'm going to buy that farm, don't you?"

"Maybe you should wait," she said. "Someone might want to surprise you with it."

Her husband, Alf, came out of the back room with Sparkles, their Yorkshire terrier. The dogs greeted each other with polite disdain. Sparkles was a bit yappy with other dogs, but Keats got a pass—probably because he considered himself a human.

Alf Halliday gave me a polite smile but then frowned when he saw the barn in my hand. "Mabel doesn't have time to make another farm before Christmas," he said. "And it's an important part of our display."

"Oh, Alf," Mabel said. "We can't stop Ivy from buying whatever she wants. Especially the farm I copied from her."

"Well, at least wait a little," he said. "It's not even Thanksgiving."

I put the barn back in its place. "Sorry, Alf."

"Shoo," Mabel said. "We don't discourage customers here at Mabel's Mutts." Her voice had a subtle note of warning that sent Alf into the back room again. "I'm so sorry, Ivy," she whispered. "Since he retired, he's been helping in the store. And he *is* a help with orders and shipping. I just wish he'd leave the front office to me."

Alf hadn't actually retired. He'd recently been part of a significant downsizing at a dairy that served all of hill country. As both a perpetrator and victim of downsizing, I understood the impact and didn't blame Mabel in the least for pretending that sharing the business was a choice. Now in his mid-fifties, Alf was unlikely to find another middle management position in a region where desk jobs were few and far between. I'd found men of his vintage took layoffs particularly hard, so I gave him full credit for feigning interest in miniature animals and villages. Mabel's smile showed more strain than it had when we met a few months ago walking our dogs in the hills. She'd loved running her own show here, and managing her husband was likely the hardest part of her job now.

"It's been quite a change and I know there's a learning curve," I said, as she used her paintbrush to point at the canister on the counter. "Kellan and I bump heads all the time and we're not even officially working together." I lifted the head off the ceramic beagle and grabbed a few liver treats. "Never will be, either. He says I can help when I graduate from the police academy."

Mabel laughed and her face relaxed. "I'm sure you can pull that off around managing your inn and far more animals than I've depicted here."

"Exactly." I couldn't tear my eyes away from the model of Runaway Farm. The inn itself was lit up from the inside. "I feel very honoured. But where's miniature Keats?"

"Boxed and under the counter waiting," she said. "It's a gift."

"What have I done to deserve such a wonderful gift?"

Mabel pushed the goggles up onto her highlighted hair and rubbed gently at the red rings they'd left around her eyes. She looked tired and Christmas was still a good way off.

"How about protecting the good people of Clover Grove from murderers?" she said. "I would think that earns a ceramic dog." Looking down at Keats, she added, "And a model dog at that." She wrinkled her nose. "Even if he does smell like... Well, I don't really know what."

"Stilton," I said. "At least according to Teri Mason. To me it's more like Gorgonzola. We visited Pages and Pastries earlier and ghosts of cheese shops past still linger."

She laughed again. "Poor Laurene. She's struggling to get things off the ground, so I pick up a coffee quite often. To go."

"The town's hard on newcomers. Even new-again people like me. I don't know how José Batista got a free pass. It seemed like people threw down the welcome mat for him."

"A red carpet, more like," Mabel said, pulling her goggles back down. "I've never seen anything like it and I've lived here all my life."

"Mom said he danced like an angel," I said. The line made my skin crawl but it was coming in quite handy. "Was he really that light on his feet?"

The goggles bobbed an affirmative. "He was, truly. At least from the few classes I attended. I'm so busy here that it was hard to get away." Now she gave me another big-eyed stare. "I heard about what happened, of course. You're taking it well."

"Better than the first time, I suppose, although it was certainly a shock." I picked up the tiny alpaca and placed her on my palm for a closer look. "I had to get away from the farm, but it wasn't really fair to abandon Jilly with the dance troupe and my mom."

"How is Dahlia doing?" Mabel dipped her brush in a little bottle of paint. "They'd become quite close, it seemed."

"Oh, you know Mom. She's never at a loss for male company, although dancers are few and far between." I set ceramic Alvina back in her pasture and picked up ceramic Drama Llama. "I think José was close to a lot of local ladies."

"Really? Who said that?"

"I could see it at the recital. Women were all atwitter. And someone down at the Berry Good Café said he was in often for tea and scones and never alone."

The goggles came up. "Are you sleuthing, Ivy? I heard José was trampled by the very llama in your hand." I clenched my fist around the tiny llama and she shook her head. "Careful, now."

"Sorry. Sorry. I break it, I buy it." Setting the llama down, I shoved my hands in my pockets. Mabel's store turned me into a kid again, and I'd never had toys like this. The fifth daughter got nothing but hand-me-downs. "There's nothing to sleuth about yet. The autopsy report won't be back until at least tomorrow. But Kellan doesn't think my animals are to blame. Perhaps you could do me a favor and send that out on the grapevine."

"That I can most certainly do." Her smile was back. "The next customer will hear it and it won't take long to circulate. But if not trampling... then what?"

I sighed. "I can only assume that after all the dancing and champagne, he made his way out to reenact the scene from the video. Maybe he had a stroke or heart attack. Kellan will get to the bottom of it. He's questioning my guests today."

She dipped the paintbrush again. "But you don't think it was natural causes, I take it."

"Well, he was a fit man."

"And if he was, well... murdered?"

"Then I would want to reassure the grapevine that my mother had nothing to do with it. She was fast asleep on the couch with Poppy when I came down this morning."

"I've known Dahlia my whole life and can't imagine her

hurting a fly. I've already said as much."

"Ah! So the grapevine is torn between blaming Alvina and Mom."

"Or both, working together." She flashed her teeth. "Can you imagine?"

I rubbed my forehead with both hands. "Mom won't get anywhere near the livestock even in daylight, which is wise, given her size. But the grapevine does like to feature her often. Easy target, I'm afraid."

"José made no secret of favouring her in class. She has so much talent." She shrugged and started painting again. "People get jealous. People get bored. Bad combination."

"Maybe someone else will take over the studio," I said. "It seems like there truly is an appetite for culture in Clover Grove."

There was a snort behind us. Alf was back in the doorway, shaking his head. "Culture? Really? You can put lipstick on a pig but it's still a pig."

"Alf! This is still my hometown, and Ivy's too. Respect, please."

I picked up the pig from the farm display and smiled. "Let's put some lipstick on Wilma and see if she classes the place up."

He forced a smile that didn't reach his eyes. "We can't afford to ruin perfectly good stock for a joke, Ivy."

"Honey," Mabel said. "Could you get me some number nine paint from the back? I'm going through white like you wouldn't believe today."

Grumbling, he retreated again and she mouthed an apology.

"No worries," I said. "Gotta run. You know full well I just came in to take the pulse on the gossip."

"I do," she said, grinning for the first time. "Don't forget

Keats."

"Forget Keats?" I looked down at the dog and saw his tail and ears had collapsed. "How could I— Oh! You mean miniature Keats."

"Less magical than the real thing, but I flatter myself I got the eyes just right."

I went around the counter and bent down to collect a little box with Keats' name on it.

There was a safety deposit box right under the till with the key sticking out of it. From that key hung a pretty blue heart with a gold letter M.

"I CAN'T BELIEVE Mabel Halliday fell for José. That is so disappointing," I told Keats as we drove home. It was late afternoon and the sun was already low. "She seems so... sensible. Like Teri."

Keats mumbled a response without turning from the road. I might be tired from a long day of poking around, but he was still raring to go.

"I probably won't ever stop being disappointed by people. I know *you* smell them for what they are, but it still takes me by surprise. Working in HR gave me a cynical shield that seems to have cracked open here. It seems strange when people keep killing people. I could use that shield more than ever."

He mumbled something that sounded like a sly dig. "No, I haven't gone soft because of Kellan, thank you very much. It's the animals. How can I stay cynical in a barn full of goodness?"

Now he sneezed, which I took as laughter and I had to join in on the joke.

"Well, Archie is good. And Alvina is good. Some of the sheep are... well, sheep. At least none of the livestock are two-faced. That's what I really mean. You know what you're getting with animals. Drama doesn't pretend to be anything other than nasty and we can work with that."

The next mumble was more like a grumble. There was no way he'd stand down on thinking the worst of Drama. Fair enough since he was on the front lines of dealing with him.

"Let's stop at Grub." I still smiled every time I said the name out loud. So many store owners missed their chance to do something fun and interesting. They were too busy chasing Dog Town's success to realize that most businesses there used tongue-in-cheek humor. Like Bone Appetit Bistro, where Bridget was the manager.

Keats' tail dropped instantly, and he whined. It didn't take any magic at all for me to know he didn't want to face Gregor, the mastiff.

"It's okay, you can guard Buttercup while I'm inside. I just need to pick up a few things. The vet left me a list and I might as well take care of it while I remember." I took my hand off the wheel and held up my palm. "Never mind. If you're going to point out that I don't want to go home, I'll just admit that straight out." I turned up the heat, which really only worked well enough to keep the windows clear. "You have no idea how much I hate that I hate going home."

His mumble turned sympathetic. He did know that, and the brief touch of his nose on my cold hand sent a wave of warmth through me.

"Thanks, buddy. You're absolutely right. *You're* my home. And luckily I can take you with me."

There was a little more mumbled encouragement.

"Of course. Jilly, too. And Percy."

He squeaked a protest.

"Yes, Percy. You love him, too. Don't even try billing it as a warm body on a cold day."

There was no one in the parking lot when I pulled up outside Grub. Simon Rezek was shifting 80-pound bags of dog kibble from a wheelbarrow to a pallet when I went inside. There were no frills and fine displays at Grub, but in addition to bulk food for almost every type of animal, they carried nearly everything else homesteaders and small farmers like me needed.

"Hey, Ivy. How ya doing?" Simon's smile was as wide and welcoming as ever. Was it possible the story hadn't reached them yet? Grub was located well outside of town, but it's not like they didn't have all the modern conveniences of gossip. He tossed another bag as if it were no heavier than a pillow, and it aligned perfectly with all the rest. I guess he'd been doing it long enough. Middle age hadn't slowed him down.

"Good," I said. "Mostly."

In truth, I'd deflated a bit. Normally my game face was reliable but the day had pushed past its limits.

Gregor trotted past me, all 110 pounds of him, and stood at the door. His hackles rose as he stared out, and I had no doubt that Keats' hackles had done the same inside Buttercup.

"I don't know what's with those two," Simon said. "Gregor's normally such a sweetheart." My expression must have shown skepticism because he added, "I couldn't have him loose in a feed store if he wasn't now, could I?"

"I guess not. Like you said at the recital, dogs will be dogs."

He blew out a breath and shook his head. "The recital. Yeah. I just want to forget that. I mean, except for the sandwiches. I'll put up with a lot for peanut butter and banana pinwheels." He walked around the counter and took the list from my hand. "It makes no sense but roll-ups just taste better."

"No argument there," I said.

Anne Rezek emerged from the cat supply section. Her arms rose as if she considered hugging me but then dropped again. Either she sensed I wasn't a fan of casual hugging or the smell of Gorgonzola really carried.

"I'm surprised you're out and about, Ivy. It must be chaos at the inn today."

"It is. Or so I've heard." I held up my cell. "Mom calls about every half hour to complain about something. Specifically, she feels like a prisoner instead of a guest. I guess Jilly's too busy to wait on her hand and foot."

Simon and Anne exchanged looks, probably over the word prisoner. Maybe they'd been speculating about how Mom might end up a prisoner for real this time.

Waving the list, Simon switched places with his wife. "Let me hunt this stuff down for you. Some things I have in stock and I'll order the rest."

Gregor clicked off behind him, and once they were out of earshot, Anne pushed her gossamer hair behind one ear and leaned across the counter. "I'm so sorry about what happened, Ivy. I don't believe a word about what people are saying. I've spent plenty of time around llamas and donkeys and they're only nasty in self-defense."

"Exactly," I said. That wasn't true of Drama Llama, but he'd likely been abused in his former life, like most of my livestock.

"So maybe José was baiting them. Like bullfighting or something. Were the animals okay?"

I nodded. "Senna came by and checked them head to toe. Or hoof, according to species. She confirmed they weren't harmed in any way. Nor did they show signs of harming anyone."

Anne studied me as if logging every word to report later. "That must be such a relief. But what really happened, then? People say it was foul play." She looked over my shoulder for her husband and then whispered, "José was such a lovely man. I can't imagine anyone wishing him ill."

"The autopsy isn't back yet, so we don't know anything more." I leaned wearily against the counter. "But I do know that people get pushed past their breaking point sometimes without ever showing signs to the rest of us. That's the real wonder. How do they hide the cracks so well?"

She nodded and her hair caught the light. I could only hope my hair would look like that one day, but I doubted it. The women in my family got wiry strands in plain old gray, rather than sleek silver.

"I have the feeling this is going to expose plenty of cracks in our community," she said. "Maybe more than... than the others. José was revered, unlike Lloyd Boyce."

"Revered. That's an interesting word. I wonder why. I mean, other than his heavenly dancing. I hear it was like being in the arms of an angel."

"I wouldn't know about that, not being a dancer. But everyone says he could make a lady feel quite special." She glanced around at the tall stacks of feed. "It's hard to feel special in Clover Grove, at least for women of a certain age." She forced a smile. "Your mom seems to defy that."

"She works hard at making herself feel special these days," I said, grinning. "But remember, it hasn't always been that way."

"Well, I didn't know her back then. I'm an import to Clover Grove, remember."

We both laughed. I knew Anne had moved here after

meeting Simon at an agricultural fair more than two decades ago, yet the town still made her feel like an outsider sometimes.

"What are you two giggling about?" Simon asked, coming back with a couple of plastic bags swinging from his hand.

"Clover Grove politics," Anne said, with a sweet smile for her husband. There was none of the tension between them that I'd felt earlier with Mabel and Alf. I supposed they'd worked together so long that they'd found their stride. "You know the rumor mill."

"Only what I hear from you, baby doll," he said. "Thank goodness I never had an ear for languages like gossip."

I took the bags from his hand. "What do I owe you?"

"I'll add it to your tab," he said. "We're missing the cat feeder, the henhouse water heater, the trimmers and the dog coat. I'll drop them by when they come in so Keats doesn't need to be stressed out by Gregor."

"Meaning he wants to come by and try to understand the mysterious language of gossip," Anne said, sliding an arm around her husband's waist.

He kissed her forehead and it gave me a sharp little pang in my chest. I missed Kellan, yet we'd seen each other only that morning. One day, I hoped we'd have the easy comfort the Rezeks shared. It took a bond like that to shield against the Joe Barkers of the world, and they were probably all the closer for not having kids.

At the door I turned back to wave and saw Gregor had wedged himself between them. Anne and Simon each rested one hand on his cropped ears. The dog wasn't much to look at, in my humble opinion, but there was a lot to be said for loyalty.

And I'd been wrong, apparently. They most certainly had a kid.

CHAPTER FIFTEEN

B y the time I turned into the lane to Runaway Farm, my breathing was steady enough to please even Jilly, the yoga devotee. Stopping at Grub had done wonders to restore my equilibrium. The Rezeks were as curious as anyone else about what happened to José, but I sensed that they truly wished me—and the entire farm—well. Sometimes it seemed like Clover Grove preferred gossip to genuine community.

"It's boredom," I told Keats, as we drove under the sign that said "Runaway Far," because the "m" had rusted out. "They need more positive distractions, like the culture revival project. Hazel says activities like that truly build connection and I'm going to take her word for it. This town could be great, you know?"

Keats' mumble sounded doubtful.

"Oh, come on. There are lots of good people just trying to find their way among the nasties. Like daisies pushing their way through concrete. We need to give them something positive to come together and root for. And in the meantime, we'll have fun."

His next mumble sounded like a "knock yourself out."

"Fine," I said. "I don't blame you for being a little skeptical after what's happened to us. And I'm counting on you, and plenty of hard work, to keep me grounded. Bringing in the livestock and putting them to bed will get us back on track."

His tail waved harder the closer we got. As much as he enjoyed a good mission, he enjoyed coming home to do his real job. He wanted to get on track, too.

Percy landed on the hood of the car before I turned off the motor. His mouth opened in what appeared to be an endless string of complaints about being left behind. The indignant parade of orange fluff in front of the windshield said it all.

"Give him a little run tonight, will you?" I asked Keats, as I turned to reach for the bags in the back seat. "We're a team and I have to keep everyone feeling happy and included."

His white front paws danced on the old leather seats. The cows, sheep and goats were still in their pastures. There was no time for indulging jealous cats.

"Percy, my friend," I said, getting out of the car. "Thank you so much for looking after everyone all day. Obviously you have plenty to tell me."

He meowed plaintively all the way into the barn and then out to the pasture, where I unlatched the gates for Keats. The dog could take it from there. All I had to do was open the doors to the various stalls inside. We'd have a very full house tonight, because the camelids and donkeys were already inside—and grumpy about it, judging by the grunts, groans and grumbles.

Drama Llama was worse than grumpy. He was so irritable about the situation that he lunged at me when I passed. Just a few more inches and he could have caught my ponytail, which wouldn't have ended well for me at all.

"Stop that," I said, glaring at him. "I don't like this any more than you do. Poor Alvina, having to put up with a grouch like you."

The alpaca was standing in the corner, looking utterly miserable. Unlike her cellmates, she was highly sensitive. Senna had told me alpacas would pine away and die without companionship, particularly from other camelids, but it didn't seem like this testy group was a great fit for Alvina.

"Maybe I should get another alpaca," I mused aloud.

There was a laugh behind me. "Really? You need more animals?"

I turned and saw Collin in the doorway. So much for a half hour of solitude before going inside.

"Well, there's always room for more in my heart, if not my barn," I said. "How are you holding up, Collin?"

He pushed back the hood of his parka and gave me a pleasant smile. "Pretty good, all things considered. Jilly is a wonderful host, and your mother... well, she keeps things lively."

"She certainly does. Your dance partners are quite lively, too."

His smile vanished. "So it seems. I had no idea that José had generated such..."

"Competition?" I suggested.

"Jealousy," he said. "Women always gravitated to him, of course, but there was no shortage of dance partners for me. Second best was still pretty great." His smile reappeared. "Most men don't see what they're missing with ballroom dance. It's done wonders for my ego. And my fitness."

He followed me as I moved from stall to stall opening doors. I repeatedly ushered him to safety so he wouldn't get caught up in the thundering hooves when Keats brought in the animals. There was one scary moment when the goats broke rank, but Collin had some footwork almost as fancy as Keats' and it ended just fine.

As I carried buckets of feed, Collin kept up a running monologue about the day. Meanwhile Percy carried on a monologue of his own. Finally the cat got so fed up with sharing the spotlight that he climbed onto a stall and prepared to launch at Collin.

"Percy, don't," I said. "Collin, look sharp. There's competition down here as well."

"What's wrong with Alvina?" he asked. "She doesn't look happy."

"She's not." I pulled out my phone and sent a quick text. "All the disruption unsettled her and she doesn't like being trapped inside with Drama. I've just asked my brother to stop by and cheer her up."

"Is there anything I can do?" He flapped his arms in Alvina's general direction. If she noticed, she didn't show it.

"This is a case for Asher, I'm afraid. Alvina develops strong monogamous attachments. She was depressed when I moved here because the former owner's husband was her first true love. Asher persisted with her, and finally she came out of her funk."

"Is that normal? I mean, for an alpaca to fall for a human like that?"

I shrugged. "What's normal with rescues? I don't have a single animal here without a sad, abnormal past. I wish that weren't true, but I hope they'll settle down eventually, knowing how loved they are."

Florence, the blind mare, grabbed the fur trim on Collin's parka and pulled. He let out a squawk and I bopped the horse's muzzle till she let go.

"There are land mines everywhere," he said, reeling back and into range of Drama.

Now Keats was on the job, however, and herded Collin out of harm's reach. Unlike Kellan, Collin found the dog's moves quite funny and turned it into a little game. Keats indulged him for a few minutes, and then cut away gracefully to chase Percy. His tail was high as they pelted out of the barn.

"I love it here," Collin said, as I walked around him to deliver hay to the cattle.

"At Runaway Farm?" I asked, brightening. I couldn't hear that often enough from guests. Kind words had been in shorter supply than murders, unfortunately.

"Yes, and Clover Grove is charming, too. I'll definitely come back after this... situation... is resolved."

"It can't happen too soon," I said. "You really heard nothing at all last night? No one going in or out?"

He shook his head. "I was tired and a little tipsy, if you must know. Slept like the dead." His eyes widened. "Sorry. Tactless."

"And you were the last to go up?" I wondered why he didn't think to get out of my way. It just made a long day longer to walk around him.

"Except for Dahlia and Poppy, yeah. The next thing I heard was your mom hollering. Her scream is like a spike in the ear."

"I've heard it," I said, forcing a smile. It was taking all my energy to keep up the front now. The sleuth simply drained out of me watching Alvina try to make herself smaller and smaller in the stall. I had more than an inkling of how she felt. Why couldn't things just be... easier?

"Excuse me." There was another voice that was less a spike in the ear than a heavy blunt instrument. Edna and her attitude managed to take up the entire doorway. "Young man, you are supposed to remain in the house at all times unless accompanied by a designated caregiver."

I smothered a laugh at her terminology. Collin had to be close to 50, but to Edna he was no different from all the kids she'd hunted down to vaccinate at school.

"Yes, Miss Evans," he said, without a trace of sarcasm. "I just needed a breath of fresh air."

"Fresh air is allowed and condoned," she said. "In the company of a caregiver. Now, let's march. Leave Ivy to get the animals settled. There's a roaring fire inside and a room full of bickering dancers. What more could you want?"

Collin squared his shoulders. "Yes, ma'am. Coming, ma'am."

"Ivy, I'll thank you to relieve me of duty soon," she said. "It's been a long day and an old woman wants her own bed."

"Yes ma'am," I said, as she circled around me to herd Collin outside.

Drama Llama reached out to snatch Edna's camouflage toque. She swept it off and whacked him on the shoulder. "Take that, you feisty beast." She winked at me as she turned. "Takes one to know one."

Finally, I was alone with only Keats, Percy and dozens of animals for company. I thought about lying down on the pile of clean hay in the corner but I was afraid I'd never get up again. Instead, I grabbed my spade and went outside. Keats grumbled to let me know that he, for one, wanted dinner.

"Just a few minutes," I said. "Before I go inside I need to hit something. Hard."

There was nothing more therapeutic in a mood like that than smashing a spade into a pile of manure. Even in cooler weather it needed to be turned because it retained more heat than soil did. That said, the work was getting harder and harder. Tonight it was exactly what I needed. There was no

way I could play the hospitable innkeeper before, well...
hitting something.

A few minutes turned into more and I'd found a good
groove when another voice rang out. "Ivy. Enough already."

It *was* enough. Just. I drove the spade into the manure
with my boot one last time and left it there. Then I jumped
down and let Kellan sweep me into his arms. He hugged me
hard, and for a few blissful moments I truly felt at home.
Safe. Instead of having to watch over everyone and everything, I could let him watch over me.

Finally I eased away, reminding myself that there would
be time for that later. It wasn't wise to let down my guard.
There was a killer on the loose and as much as Kellan might
want to protect me, he couldn't keep every last furry or feath-
ered head on my property safe. He was carrying a heavy load,
too. If the farm felt like a big responsibility, an entire community must feel massive. I wondered if I'd fully appreciated the
weight of his job until that moment.

"You okay?" he asked, as I steadied myself and looked up.
His face was as handsome as ever but the spark of fun was
understandably gone from his eyes tonight. I missed that
spark. It kept the fire burning in my heart, when I wanted
to... well, hit things.

"Yeah. It's just been a day, you know?"

Now he smiled. "It has indeed. What a bunch of fire-
crackers in there. Can't you find some dull guests?"

"I keep hoping for a staid book club. That's my dream. To
sit around shooting the breeze about Jane Austen or the
Bronte sisters."

"Stamp collectors," he suggested. "Or coins. Super dull,
probably."

"You'd think so, but bridge turned out to be incendiary,

didn't it? Seems like everyone gets fired up when they land here. Must be something in the water."

"Or the manure," he suggested, taking a step back. "If you don't mind my saying, you have something extra going on in the perfume department."

I laughed. "Sorry about that."

"What kind of sleuthing could you possibly have been doing that would leave you smelling worse than manure therapy?"

"Sleuthing? What do you mean?" I scuffed my boot on the hard earth. "I was just running errands in smelly places."

"Ivy. I thought we weren't going to pretend anymore. You're going to do what you do without getting yourself or anyone else killed and I'm going to grin and bear it." He sighed. "Make that grimace and bear it. Because obviously I'd prefer you didn't."

I stood on tiptoe and leaned forward to kiss his cheek, keeping a little distance for the sake of his nose. "All my stops were in public and broad daylight. I just wanted to chat to some of the women from José's dance class, because I noticed at the recital they were seething with jealousy—just like the women here. That man overwhelmed sensible women and opened their wallets, Kellan. He must have built quite a stash. Where is it?"

Kellan shrugged. "I barely got through questioning the dancers here, today. I hope you have flood coverage because the tears really flowed. All of them contributed to José's fund at some time, too, and they didn't even hold a grudge that he left their towns and moved on. There was no bitterness toward him—only each other, and particularly your mom, who was considered the frontrunner in the race to get the man to settle down. At the same time, they hoped she could pull it off, so he'd stop rolling on. I think they'd have moved here just to be in his orbit."

"I don't get it," I said. "Jilly and I felt none of that magnetic pull. He just seemed like an average Joe to me."

Kellan smiled at the joke. "You and Jilly are not average women."

"And we didn't dance with him. That's where the real damage happened, Kellan. He swept women away by making them feel special. Life here can be a lonely slog and he made them feel light and lovely. It was addictive, I suppose, and they wanted to help fund his studio so they could hold onto the feeling. I'm not sure anything more salacious was going on."

"He did the same in many other towns," Kellan said. "And got away with it, too. We'll never know the full scope because only a fraction of the scammed women will admit to donating. He left a trail of broken leases almost as long as the trail of broken hearts."

I crossed my arms and hugged myself since I didn't want to impose my cheesy perfume on him. "But how will the killer ever be found? Someone with a grudge could have followed him from any of his previous stops."

"Let's hope so, because outsiders are often easier to find than locals. They don't know how to hide their tracks in a small community like this one." Suddenly he looked around, as if sensing four eyes upon him. Keats and Percy had gotten into position for a double ambush and both looked utterly crestfallen when he shook his finger at them. "Find another victim, boys. I've had a day, too. I'll cuff you both and cart you away if there's so much as a hair on my uniform."

That was a lost cause, as a film of fuzz and dust had settled over him already. Still, I was grateful to the dog and cat for lightening the mood.

"So you're thinking it's a local?" I asked. "A jealous spurned woman?"

"Probably," he said. "I need the autopsy report, but it looks like the killer used a smaller blade, which could be consistent with a female killer. José was slight, but it's still not easy for a woman to take down a man."

"He was tipsy and easier to tip," I said. "Mom said they all were."

Kellan nodded. "So it's just a matter of figuring out which of the many women he deceived went over the edge."

"Well, I can tell you one thing to look for," I said, pulling out my phone and flashing him a photo of Teri's private collection. "José had these made and gave them to his most devoted supporters. I've already tracked down the L, the M and the T," I continued. "Laurene Pedal from Pages and Pastries, Mabel Halliday, and Tish Ramsey. "It seemed like Tish had the most to lose. Her engagement to Ryan Snopes is at risk over that money. Oh, and Keats growled at her, too."

"Case closed then," Kellan said, grinning as he took my hand and led me away from the manure and back into the barn. "If Keats hates her, we all hate her."

"I love it when you talk that way," I said, before abruptly yanking him out of Drama Llama's reach. "I'll keep looking around for the key fobs with the J, N and B."

He didn't tell me I couldn't, as I'd expected. Instead he stared into Alvina's pen. "What's with her? She looks so sad."

I nodded. "She likes routine and there's been constant upheaval since the video shoot. It's going to take a serious intervention by Asher to shift this mood."

"You can take her back outside tomorrow," he said. "We finished up quickly because it's going to rain overnight and wash away any evidence."

"That'll help," I said. "It's so hard when your animals suffer and you don't know what to do."

Kellan pulled me over and hugged me again. "On second thought," he murmured in my ear, "you smell just about perfect."

CHAPTER SIXTEEN

Jilly practically skipped ahead of me to Buttercup the next day. Daisy had agreed to stay at the inn for the morning to give Jilly a break from the guests' incessant pleas to clear out the family room again and dance. While we understood it would be a great stress reliever, dancing didn't seem entirely appropriate, given what had happened. It was also the kind of thing that would feed the rumor mill. People would say we were dancing on the poor man's grave. There wasn't much I could do to control gossip except calling a moratorium on the mambo until things settled down. By then, hopefully this group would be so tired of our company they'd want to head home. It was a shame most of our guests to date had been ecstatic to leave, but eventually the tide would turn. Or so I hoped, because it would be pretty much impossible to find a "real job" in hill country to support this place.

"Why Buttercup?" Jilly asked, sliding into the passenger seat. "Have you given up on the truck completely?"

She didn't notice Percy darting in behind her. I considered evicting the stowaway as our mission wasn't cat-friendly today, but he'd become a master of evasion under the seats. The time I'd spend lying in the rear footwell and poking him out with a hiking pole would be stressful for both of us. If he wanted to cool his heels in the car with Keats while Jilly and I lunched, then let him. Maybe he'd think twice the next time.

"Nope. I wanted to take some lessons after the last... deadly incident. But before I could get around to it, the next incident happened. The beauty of Buttercup—and I don't say this lightly—is that driving her frees my mind to ponder the great mysteries of farm life. The gearshift requires my full attention."

Jilly laughed as Buttercup chugged and lurched down the lane. She wasn't a morning car, or a cold weather car. It would be half an hour till she was in the mood to indulge us with a smooth ride, let alone heat. One of Jilly's jobs as passenger was to keep the windshield clear. She kept a small towel handy to wipe the old girl down like a boxer between rounds. That meant Keats was a hindrance in her lap but it didn't stop him from trying.

"Wouldn't it be nice to have a normal vehicle?" Jilly asked. "Yours are as eccentric as some of your rescues. It's all about indulging their idiosyncrasies."

"That's an astute observation, my friend." I made sure the coast was clear to turn onto the highway. At Buttercup's pace, I needed extra space to ease into traffic. "I hate to say a good word about Flordale Corp, but at least working in that cutthroat environment taught me to indulge personalities and whims."

"Not to mention preparing you for an *actual* cutthroat environment," Jilly said. "It never seemed like readiness training for murder investigation, but looked how it turned out."

"Good point. You can help me position that properly on my résumé when it comes time to find another full-time job."

She squeezed my right arm while continuing to fend off Keats' incursions between the seats. "Don't say that. The murders have got to stop. Like your mom says, it's just not sustainable."

"Let's smudge the place with sage again. There's some bad juju that needs to be cleared if we're ever to get the average, boring guests we need to thrive here."

"Agreed. We'll do a big smudge before the snow flies. Let's borrow Edna's ATV and do the full property."

I glanced at her and grinned. "You're itching to get on that dune buggy, aren't you?"

Jilly laughed. "Is it that obvious? It just looks so fun. Edna is having the time of her life."

"She might be the only one who doesn't mind some bloodshed in the neighborhood. Keeps things interesting." I turned off the main highway and took the bypass toward Dorset Hills. "All those years spent spying have paid off. It must be so validating for her."

"As annoying as Edna is, she was a huge help yesterday. She patrolled the inn constantly, inside and out, and if guests made a misstep, she reminded them she was packing."

"Seriously? She told them she was armed? That's not the kind of thing we want in reviews."

"Not normally, but I honestly think it helped everyone feel more at ease knowing Edna would use her arsenal in their defense, too. She was clearly itching to deploy, but no one gave her an opportunity."

I risked taking my hand off Buttercup's vibrating steering wheel to rub my forehead. "I don't know whether to laugh or cry."

"Laugh, my friend. Whatever happens, we try to laugh, remember?"

It was a commitment we'd made in college when we instantly recognized the kindred spirit in each other. Back in those giddy days, we got kicked out of class often for doing that very thing. Once we started laughing, it was nearly impossible to quit. Little did we know that too was training for life ahead. I suppose if you tried hard enough, you could see—or manufacture—a reason for everything. But one thing I never questioned was my good luck in meeting Jilly that day. She asked me to move my bag off a chair in a crowded cafeteria and within five minutes we were giggling over something. The rest was history.

"I remember well," I said. "In fact, I believe all the laughing increased my cardiovascular capacity. Without that, I probably couldn't handle the rigors of farm work, let alone sleuthing."

"See, there's the Ivy I love and admire. Always trying to turn a sow's ear into a silk purse." She paused. "Are we allowed to use expressions like that now? As farmers? It sounds inhumane."

"In the confines of Buttercup, anything goes. Let's make that our new rule. I am trying to blurt less in public."

"And making very good progress," she said. "You'll have a chance to practice tonight at the first culture-raising meeting. I'm glad Edna's freeing us up to attend. She finds the whole idea of culture nauseating. I think her clash with the Bridge Buddies put her off joining anything but other preppers."

"It's just as well. She seems more comfortable in fatigues now and that'll fuel chatter."

Hazel Bingham had thrown open the doors of her old manor to host the first gathering because we couldn't do it at the inn. I knew she was also trying to create an opportunity for me to study local suspects and I appreciated that. Since I'd helped solve a crime in her family, she was committed to backing me in anything I needed. I was learning to look for the flowers of friendship blooming in unusual places. Come to think of it, sunflowers in a derelict back yard had attracted me to Keats.

He rested his muzzle on my shoulder now and mumbled something.

"We're almost there," Jilly said, answering his question. "But you need to stay in the car, my friend. Cold weather has closed the patios."

Keats retreated and collapsed into a sulk in the back seat. His ears lifted slightly when Percy came out and draped his orange fluff across the black-and-white of Keats' coat.

We were in Dog Town proper now, and the big bronze statues that characterized the place were hard to ignore even in heavy traffic. A dozen blocks showcased nearly 20 breeds. I looked for the parking lot near City Hall with the eight-foot-high West Highland terrier. Evie Springdale had assured me there was always plenty of room for a big, moody car like Buttercup. Sure enough, there was a wide spot in a sunny corner that was perfect. I tried to pat Keats but he ducked away from my hand.

"Love you, buddy," I said. "I'll eat fast, I promise."

Evie had asked us to meet her at The Puccini Café, a cute little place not far from City Hall and Bingham Square, with the huge bronze German shepherd guardian. Her message had been deliberately vague and I hadn't pressed. As a former political public relations expert, Evie knew what to say and when, so I was content to let things unfold.

She had arrived early to get the corner seat in the café and waved eagerly as we walked in. Despite the urgent rescue work the Mafia got called upon to do unannounced,

Evie usually looked stylish. She kept a change of clothes in her trunk and could slip into rescue gear in the back seat in record time. I wondered if I should do the same with more presentable clothing and learn to switch out of overalls when the occasion required. On the bright side, I firmly believed my farm couture kept people's guard down and loosened their tongues.

Evie hugged Jilly and I decided to relax my personal space rules and allow a quick one, too. Most of the Mafia weren't huggers, but Evie and Remi Malone seemed to hold their arms in perpetual readiness. No doubt Jilly and I looked like we needed one today.

The waiter took our order, and while we waited for the food to arrive, Evie pulled out her tablet to show us some of the footage from José's last official performance. She tried to fast forward past him to Alvina's closeups but I took the tablet to study the master dancer, and even blew up the image.

"I still don't get it," I said. "What is that man's appeal?"

"Presence," Evie said. "I've worked with enough politicians to know. When José danced with someone the world dropped away. He made them feel light and graceful and elegant, like he was. Even the men felt a buzz being around him. It's obvious from the footage."

I handed the tablet back. "I guess he felt that entitled him to bilk people."

"Maybe they were happy to give it to him because he made them feel great," Evie said.

"But they couldn't spare it, which makes it unethical," I said. "That's what really bothers me. He wasn't going after the big fish who could afford it, but the little guys."

"That's where you're wrong," Evie said. "He went after big fish, too. José cast his hook widely."

The food arrived and she fell silent till the waiter left. I couldn't take a bite of my grilled cheese sandwich with Evie's own hook dangling, so I bit. "Come on, Evie. Tell us."

She speared a couple of fries and chewed before answering. "Eat your fries while they're hot," she said, pushing the ketchup toward me. My cheeks warmed too as I recalled how the Mafia had found me nearly kissing Kellan at the Bone Appetit Bistro with my chest pressed into the condiments. I'd ruined Jilly's second-best sweater but also entered a new stage in my relationship, so I had no real regrets.

When my mouth was full of fries, I mumbled, "*Now*, tell us."

After checking for eavesdroppers, Evie said, "Check out the woman at the cash register. Turn one at a time and don't make it obvious."

The woman was middle aged and as well preserved as Mom. Her hair and makeup were so polished that the apron looked out of place.

"That's the owner?" I asked.

Evie nodded. "The new owner. Recently divorced by a longtime city councillor. When we ousted the corrupt mayor, a lot of the old boys left, too. Or got nudged out by Isla, our new mayor. As soon as this guy was done, he cut ties with his wife. The optics didn't matter once he was back running a law firm. So he bought this place out from under the old owner and set his ex up here."

"That's interesting," Jilly said, poking at her food. The sandwich and fries tasted great to me, but my foodie friend had a finicky palate. "I have the feeling there's more to the story."

"You're so right," Evie said, pointing her fork at Jilly. "According to the Dog Town rumor mill, which is just as robust as Clover Grove's and much faster, this woman had an affair last year." She paused for dramatic effect. "With a ball-room dancer."

I dropped my fork and then stilled it before the clatter attracted attention. "Joe Barker hit Dog Town?"

"Indeed he did. He rented out studio space in Riverdale and had a following in no time. Word of mouth pulled in the councillor's wife and next thing you know, José's lease was terminated for a long list of supposed violations and he was driven out of town. You didn't mess with the last mayor or his cronies. Careers were ruined for less."

I'd heard stories and knew that the former mayor was wily and corrupt. It had taken a strong rebel faction of dog rescuers to drive him out of town. Now he was licking his wounds elsewhere, perhaps to rise again later.

"Do you have details for Kellan?" I asked.

Evie nodded. "Let's just say it wouldn't surprise me at all if the old boys' network finished off the job when they heard José had popped up again so close to home. He preyed on lonely women wherever he found them and once he'd drained the bank, moved on to the next town."

I stared at my food and it no longer looked appealing. "It disgusts me to hear that, particularly since my mom was one of his victims."

Evie reached over and touched my sleeve. "I know it's hard seeing depravity up close, but I have something to tell you, based on my long experience in politics..."

She crooked her finger. Jilly and I both leaned forward and whispered, "What?"

"Never ever let it ruin your enjoyment of good fries," she said. We both sat back, laughing. "There's a time to fight crime and a time to eat fries. That fine balance is what keeps you going."

Jilly picked up her Rueben sandwich, took a bite and

chewed. "This isn't bad, actually. I could make a version of this for the inn. Better, of course."

"I want to talk to you about the inn," Evie said. "More specifically about marketing in the face of murder. I have some ideas."

"Yes?" Jilly's voice overlapped with mine and we both leaned forward eagerly.

"Let's get the current issue out of the way and then do some brainstorming," Evie said. "How about I loop the others in, too?"

"That would be great," I said. Although I felt sheepish about needing anyone's advice on running my business, the time for pride was over. I'd take help when it was offered, at least when it came from people I trusted, including the Rescue Mafia. That's what community was all about. You just had to choose your community wisely.

After that, the food disappeared quickly and we were nearly done when there was a thud on the glass beside us.

Turning, we saw Cori Hogan with her black glove raised in a fist. She thumped the window lightly again and then unfurled her fingers to beckon. As always, the middle finger was neon orange.

Evie checked her phone, and then slid some bills across the table to me. "Can you pay while I go out to see what Cori wants?"

"Sure, but I want to know what Cori wants, too."

"What she wants first is for you to pay at the cash register," Evie said. "Apparently there's something you need to see."

I headed for the cash register and offered my best smile to the owner. It was nice for a change that someone didn't recognize me and have preconceptions. I felt 10 pounds lighter being anonymous.

The woman smiled back before turning to ring up my bill. As she moved, I noticed the key fob hanging out of the cash register: a mauve heart with a scrolly "J" encased in fake glass. The name tag pinned to her apron said Janet.

My hand shook a little as she poured the change into it and I could barely form the word yes when she asked if I'd enjoyed the meal.

I made my way outside and crossed the road to join Cori, Evie and Jilly in front of the corgi statue outside Barkingham Palace Café. I already knew this dog was a fiberglass knockoff of the sanctioned statues but couldn't resist rapping on its side anyway to hear the hollow sound. Nothing was as it seemed in Dorset Hills, either.

"How did you know about the key fobs?" I asked Cori.

The petite trainer shrugged. As usual she was dressed all in black, ready for action. No backseat changes for Cori. Where rescue was involved, every second counted. "It's my business to know things," she said. "I've trained Janet's dog, and when I heard about Joe Barker's sleazy gifts, Evie and I put two and two together."

"Does that mean the grapevine is buzzing about the key fobs? If so, I'll never find the missing ones."

Evie shook her head. "Inside knowledge, we promise. We can't divulge our sources, but take our word for it and go get this guy."

"I will," I said. "Thank you."

"No need to thank us," Cori said. "You'll do that by hosting our new rescue."

"The ark is already full," Jilly said. "I can hardly get Ivy to come inside as it is."

"That's because she doesn't want to come inside," Cori said. "Not because she's overworked."

"Tell me it's not a camel," Jilly said. "Ivy dropped that into casual conversation and I've been worried ever since."

"Not a camel," Cori said, grinning.

"Another alpaca?" I asked, hopefully. "Alvina is rattled after what happened and she doesn't seem to take comfort from the llamas or donkeys."

"Get your brother over to cut a rug," Cori said. "All she needs is some male attention. As we've seen, many females lose their minds when men dance with them."

"He's coming by today," I said. "But I'm worried about her."

"She'll be fine," Cori said. "This new rescue isn't likely to be her type, though. Charlie's already making the necessary adjustments for its rather unique needs."

Jilly's sigh sent out a big puff of frosty steam that Cori waved away with a flap of orange middle finger. "Relax, Jilly. It's temporary."

"It's always temporary... until Ivy can't part with any of them."

Cori started to walk off with Evie, offering an orange-fingered reverse wave. "That's what I like about her. But this rescue I can pretty much guarantee she'll want to give back."

"Why doesn't that make me feel any better?" Jilly asked, as we headed toward Buttercup.

"Because it's a baby dragon," I said. "And you're worried it'll burn down the farm."

"Very funny," Jilly said, laughing as she evicted Keats and Percy from the passenger seat. "Like I don't have enough nightmares already, Ivy Galloway."

Sliding behind the wheel, I grinned at her. "Let's just keep laughing, my friend. You said it first."

CHAPTER SEVENTEEN

It was lovely to see the old Bingham Manor lit up as it probably had been in its glory days. Mom was sitting in Buttercup's passenger seat, periodically swatting at Keats who was trying to work his way into her lap. Jilly had gone ahead with Asher when Mom dragged out her preparations to the point where I threatened to leave her behind. I'd already stuck my neck out just to get Kellan to agree to let her attend and had swung by her apartment earlier to collect what seemed to be half of her considerable wardrobe. It had eaten into my sleuthing time, but I'd managed to stop at Peachtree Fine Foods to encourage Ryan to come to the culture-raising meeting tonight. We needed as many of the town's key players as possible to show up if we hoped to gain any traction. Of course, I was also eager to watch Joe Barker's former fans interact with each other, particularly since Kellan was too busy with work to join us.

"Ivy, seriously," Mom said, pushing Keats back yet again. "Your dog is incorrigible. And he smells."

"He does not," I said, trying to find room to park in a very crowded yard. "Or not much. I used a special dry shampoo for dogs on him."

"So now he smells like fake flowers. It's no better than manure."

"There's no pleasing some people, Keats," I said.

"You could please me by leaving the dog at home," she said. "Not to mention the cat. I know he's in here. I can feel it."

"Percy loves visiting Hazel's," I said. "I couldn't deny him just like I couldn't deny you. Remember I had to twist Kellan's arm to bust you out of the inn."

"It's ridiculous that I have to be shut up with those people like a common criminal. The women are so catty. José —I mean, Joe—is gone, yet they're still bitter that he paid me a little extra attention. They should realize carrying resentment destroys their looks. I try to let things go for that reason alone."

"It's a good policy, whatever your motivation," I said. "Why don't you just flirt with Collin and James to keep your skills sharp until you're back on the dating circuit? They're both attractive men."

She offered a cluck of disgust. "They're José wannabes, which obviously has no appeal to me now." Percy emerged from the back to land on her shoulder and she gave a little scream. "Get your fur away from me, you cur."

"We talked about this. Only a dog can be a cur."

"Or a man," she said. "And that's why I've decided to end my rotation."

I turned off the engine and looked at her. "What? Are you feeling okay?"

"I'm fine. I just don't want to put myself in such a vulnerable position again." She pinched her cheeks to bring color and leaned over to do the same to me. I swatted at her just as she had at Keats. "I'm going to devote all my attention to my salon and my children."

My stomach lurched at that but at least the attention would be spread across six of us, and hopefully the grandsons she mostly ignored. Sweet girls she could dress up in second-hand finds would have stood a better chance of getting noticed. At least Daisy seemed content with Mom's benign neglect of her twins.

"Marketing the salon is a great idea," I said. "Maybe I could help."

"Thank you, darling, but I'm afraid your reputation will only hurt my business. The name Ivy Galloway carries instant associations with murder."

"Excuse me?" I pushed the car door open. "You're the one who hasn't been cleared of murder—so soon after being cleared of the one in your salon." I slammed the door and continued speaking as she emerged. "Your reputation doesn't help my business, either."

"Piffle," she said, easing Buttercup's door closed. "I'd thank you to be gentle with my favorite child. Buttercup never has sharp words that cut a mother's heart."

"Could you do me a favor and try not to pick any fights tonight?" I said, letting Keats and Percy take the lead to the house. "People might bait us and we need to be strong and resist... for the sake of our fresh complexions."

"I agree with you there. Plus if I resist their traps, maybe the chief will let me go back to the salon. I need to be working."

Those were words I'd rarely heard from my mom. Once my siblings and I had started financing her, most of her efforts were half-hearted at best. Before the salon launched, she mainly worked to socialize or get staff discounts.

"We're going to stick to you like burrs tonight," I said.

"Cause any trouble at all and into Buttercup you go. I won't have your antics coming between Kellan and me."

She glanced up at me with mild approval. "I'm pleased to hear you say that, Ivy. Because as much as the chief is a thorn in my side, I'd rather have him around than not. A woman can't have too many police officers in her life." In the front hall, she handed me her coat and added, "You'd do well to keep your own antics from coming between you."

I hung our coats on the last empty hook and guided Mom into the crowd. Percy slipped away immediately but I assigned Keats to keep an eye on Mom. To her great annoyance, he kept herding her back to me as she tried to mingle.

We found Hazel in the dining room, sitting at the head of the long oak table that had been a wedding gift from her grandfather to his bride.

"Hazel," I said, "you look wonderful. And happy."

She pushed her chair back and gestured to the marmalade fluff curled up on her midnight blue velvet dress. Percy always favored Hazel and she was willing to pay the price in dry cleaning.

"Ivy, I'm so sorry about what happened," she said. "But we won't speak of it tonight."

My eyes almost teared up at the kindness in her voice, but I just nodded my thanks. "Let's speak of what's happened to this table, instead. Last time I saw it the finish had taken a terrible beating from hundreds of claws."

Hazel's home had been overrun with cats for a time but she'd reclaimed it and turned it around quite quickly.

"Michael," she said, simply. "He's been coordinating contractors to restore the place. The table he refinished himself because he knew it was that important to me. Honestly, I wouldn't have hosted anyone until it was back to its former glory. Now it is."

Her nephew was at the other end of the long table describing the project to my mother, who was making a better effort than usual to feign interest in renovations.

"He's a good man," I said, raising my hand to signal Keats.

"Oh, leave it," Hazel said. "Dahlia's a pistol but Michael could use the distraction. How is she holding up?"

"Showing some wear and tear," I said. "Not literally."

In fact, Mom was wearing a red lace dress over a black slip that was quite stunning. She'd explained earlier how she stitched three separate dresses together to create it, and I'd glazed over in much the same way she was while Michael discussed sanding the old table. And, I supposed, in much the same way people glazed over when I talked about tending my livestock, or worse, my manure pile. I was hardly in a position to judge.

"I admire Dahlia's resilience," Hazel said. "I daresay it's something all four of us have in common."

I nodded. "Yet with all the challenges we've faced, we still have energy to give something back to our community. It was kind of you to open your doors to this crowd when I couldn't."

"My pleasure and civic duty," she said. "I'm one of the few who remembers this town in full splendor. I want to help restore Clover Grove, just as we're doing with this house."

Mandy McCain circulated with trays of punch and finger foods alongside a couple of young waiters I recognized from the Berry Good Café. They were all wearing white shirts, black pants and name tags. I stopped one of them to grab some punch for Mom and was shocked to find myself face-to-face with Tish Ramsey. I looked down to see if she was wearing her stilettos and was reassured to find she was.

"Punch?" she asked, with a smirk.

"Yes, thank you, Tish." I fumbled for my purse. "Let me tip you."

"That won't be necessary. Miss Bingham included a gratuity."

"I want to. I know you need—"

She turned away, saying, "I don't need anything from you, Ivy Galloway. Respect my privacy, please and thank you."

The crowd parted as she wobbled off and I saw Ryan Snopes melt away to avoid her. This must be excruciating for him, but I couldn't help but admire Tish a little for following through on her commitment to repay him.

There was clapping from a small podium near the grand fireplace in the living room. After passing the punch to Mom, I took Hazel's arm to lead her there. When we met, she'd used a walker, and then downgraded to a cane. Now she was quite steady without either one but I didn't trust the rest of the crowd not to reverse that.

Jilly was on the podium looking gorgeous in the pink dress I'd bought from Chez Belle to replace the one Drama Llama stained with spit. Her hair hung in long ringlets and I think the silence fell more from admiration than anything else. Asher stood as close as he could, staring up at her raptly. I'd worried people wouldn't take her seriously tonight—either because she was a newcomer, or because of the trouble at Runaway Farm. Clearly I'd underestimated the miracles good looks and confidence could work, even with a tough crowd.

Long before Jilly turned chef at the inn she'd held throngs like this in her sway. Corporate executives hired her to deliver motivational speeches, even though it led to losing some people, who hired Jilly afterward to place them in new jobs. Most staff just went to their own jobs more inspired to excel. She was that good.

While she commanded their attention, I looked around, trying to identify women with names that might match the missing key fobs. I was still missing the H, the B and the N. But despite knowing all the lifers and many of the newcomers, I couldn't place the likely victims of Joe Barker's so-called charms.

Tonight Jilly kept her speech short, explaining that we were forming an executive committee to oversee the Clover Grove Culture Revival Project. Our goal was to enlist people to share their expertise and introduce locals to new interests and hobbies. There was no pressure and no cost. If all went as planned, they'd learn something, have fun and make like-minded friends. When she called for volunteers a dozen hands flew up.

Iris was the first to speak, offering sessions about hill country history and guided tours of the dozens of small museums in the region. People applauded and my sister, the shyest Galloway Girl, flushed bright red.

Teri Mason was quick to offer both art appreciation tours at local galleries and craft classes at the store. Mabel Halliday followed with an offer to give free hands-on pottery and ceramics lessons. Her husband glowered behind her, probably to protest doing anything for free in the busiest season of the year.

Jilly offered cooking classes at the inn and while there was a murmur of unrest, people couldn't resist either their curiosity or the lure of her cuisine. The applause brought a smile to her face and an even bigger one to Asher's. He followed by proposing self defense classes and while that didn't necessarily qualify as "culture," it was an excellent idea.

And so it went, with offers from Laurene Pedal to run a book club, Kaye Langman to lead Antiques 101, and Mandy to offer baking basics. Someone I hadn't met pledged to start a choir, someone else a string quartet and yet another a jazz band. Ryan Snopes volunteered to share advice on making the most of local produce and backyard bounty.

Many of the sessions sounded fun to me, which was promising, since I'd normally rather shovel manure than socialize.

Simon and Anne Rezek waited for the flurry to calm down before raising their hands at the same time. He grabbed hers, laughing, and then offered to host information nights at Grub for livestock hobbyists. Local home-steaders were quickly expanding beyond their backyard henhouses and needed advice, particularly with winter coming. Simon had downgraded a large farm operation in recent years and knew his topic well. Those were sessions I wouldn't miss.

Voices began to blur together and my head started pounding. I could only handle so much hubbub before my concussion reminded me it hadn't fully healed. As if by magic, Keats appeared at my side and shoved his head under my fingertips.

"Thanks, buddy," I whispered. The dog had cleverly herded Mom to Asher, which left me free to grab some fresh air. I let Keats guide me, and eventually Percy, into the back-yard. It was a clear night, with a billion pretty stars gleaming overhead and a breeze so cold it could collapse a lung. I shiv-ered, less from the wintry gust than the chilling memory of what we'd discovered here weeks ago. Keats leaned against me in sympathy, but Percy scaled the lattice fence at the side of the porch. The cat's tail puffed suddenly and caused me to freeze in a different way.

"I told you I didn't want to see you," a man's voice said, on the other side of the lattice. "Yet here you are."

"You told me to pay you back, and here I am."

It was Ryan and Tish, arguing again.

"And I told you I could never buy back the trust of the community. I'll have to do that with free classes for the rest of my life. Trust is the only way to survive in a town like this."

"It's the only way to survive in a relationship too," Tish said. "I'm trying to regain yours by serving punch to the people who don't trust you."

There was a pause before he said, "You just don't get it, Tish. This is my home, where I grew up, and where I was once—"

"The high school football hero. I know. I get it."

"You don't, though," he said. "You don't get what respect is all about."

"And you don't get what compromise is all about. Do you think I want to serve punch? I'm a beautician. I broke a nail tonight."

"It's time we took a break, Tish. Unless you can fix what you *really* broke."

"Me? You're the one who broke everything, Ryan. It's on you to fix it as much as me. We're in this together."

I looked down at Keats and saw that his tail was stiff, his hackles up and his ears back. We weren't safe, even with a crowd inside. I backed slowly to the door, desperately trying to catch Percy's eye without making a sound. Finally the cat glanced back and his green eyes stared past me to the other side of the patio. Something crackled in the bushes there, and Keats let out a low growl.

"Boys, inside," I whispered, so low it was practically just a thought. Soon we were surrounded by people again but it was a long time before I stopped shivering.

CHAPTER EIGHTEEN

"Darling, what's wrong?" Mom asked, while we drove down Hazel's lane. "You're acting like you saw a ghost."

"I feel like it," I said. "I shouldn't have gone outside. It reminded me of discovering those old bones."

"Best to bury old bones like bad memories," Mom said. "I know that's hard to do sometimes. We both have our work cut out for us."

I murmured agreement and Keats rested his muzzle on my shoulder, trying to infuse me with warmth. Percy slid through the impossibly narrow space on the other side of the passenger seat and wormed his way into Mom's lap. Instead of evicting him she actually stroked him and a purr boomed out that rivaled Buttercup's moody motor.

"How come you didn't offer sewing classes?" I asked. "You have a talent for design that should be shared."

"Redesign," she corrected. "That's not valued, I'm afraid. Even with the emphasis on recycling and refurbishing in this town, people prefer new clothes." She shrugged and smiled. "That leaves the best finds to me."

"Well then, you could teach barbershop basics. That could attract some new clients to the salon. If not dates for your rotation."

"Perhaps, when all this blows over." She waved her hand as if to dispel a smell. "Murder casts such a pall over everything, doesn't it?"

"It most certainly does. If it's killed your desire to date, that's monumental."

She let that slide for a moment or two before saying, "I wouldn't say killed, necessarily. I'm just going to proceed with great caution. Michael and I are having dinner when I'm released from lockdown at the inn."

"Michael? As in Michael Bingham, Hazel's nephew?"

"Michael Bingham who refurbished that gorgeous table. Yes."

"Mom! He's fresh out of a shattered marriage."

"Oh, darling." She waved her hand again and this time I was the metaphorical stink. "It's dinner, that's all."

"Dating him is sheer madness, even for you."

She actually laughed—her good laugh, the melodious one. "Ivy, really. You're overreacting. It's one dinner. If he passes the audition into my rotation, we'll worry about it then."

"There's no way he's ready to date. It's been weeks since his trust was utterly destroyed. Not months. Not years. *Weeks*."

"Exactly. Michael is on the rebound, which makes him ideally suited to a rotation. He's the epitome of emotionally unavailable. As I've told you before, men of my age tend to be clingy. They want someone to take care of them. Clearly, that's not me."

"Because *you're* emotionally unavailable."

She turned to stare at the side of my head. The impact

was lost in the darkness but Keats gave her face a big slurp, a rare gift for a woman he loved. Plucking my hat from between the seats, she used it to pat her face gently.

"Michael seems quite lovely," she said. "And normal."

"How normal can he be after what he's been through?"

"How normal can you and I be after what we've been through?" she countered. "And yet we date. We have hope that better things await. It really is all about hope, isn't it?"

I wanted to argue but hope for better things was exactly what kept me going, especially with Kellan. I was far from normal and yet he gave me a chance.

"Well, please be kind to him, Mom. He's a decent man and Hazel is a good friend to me. I don't have that many."

"Like I said, it's just dinner. And in accepting him, I decided to resume my full rotation. I think it's the only way to heal my wounds after what happened with José. I mean, Joe." Her hand stroked Percy from head to tail a few times before she continued. "The whole thing rattled me. How could I have been so terribly wrong about a man?"

Her last word, "again," was barely audible.

"Mom, you weren't alone. Many smart, sensible women fell for Joe's ploy. You'll hear more when Kellan is ready to share." I eased my foot off the gas to slow our roll. "Some fell much harder than you did and paid a higher price for it."

"Really?" Her voice brightened. "I mean, I don't like knowing other women were swindled, but I want to believe I gained *something* from the lessons your father taught me. This incident made me doubt."

"Did he—my father—swindle you?" I asked.

She didn't answer for a while and I slowed the car even more to give her time. "I never wanted to badmouth him to you kids," she said at last. "He was still your father, and I wasn't sure if he'd reappear in your lives someday. He had problems, Ivy. A difficult childhood. Dreadful parents. Trouble in school." She reached over her shoulder for Keats and stroked his head with her left hand and Percy with her right. "None of that excuses leaving us virtually penniless and living in shame in a small community. And yes, he drained what savings we had to get a fresh start." After another long pause, she added, "With a new woman. One of the younger ones."

I knew some of this, albeit vaguely. I was a small child when he left and people only talked about it when they thought I couldn't hear. So I allowed myself to not know, at least officially.

"I'm sorry that happened to you," I said.

"And I'm sorry it happened to *you*. And that I couldn't stop it."

I thought about asking more but decided that was about all I could handle hearing right now, and probably all she could handle sharing. We'd just been through another trauma and needed time to recover. If the story had waited this long, it could wait some more.

We were almost at the turnoff to Runaway Farm when Mom said, "Keats? Should I tell her?"

He mumbled a quick and decided affirmative.

"Maybe not," I said. "We're almost home. I'm not sure I want to know more about my deadbeat father."

"It's not about that. I just wanted to mention I have a key to José's dance studio."

I hit the brakes so hard Buttercup almost bucked us into the ditch at the side of the road. Mom used one hand to brace herself on the dash and the other to hold Percy.

"Did you tell Kellan?" I asked.

"Not yet. My policy in these matters is to answer what's asked and only what's asked. He didn't ask."

I steered Buttercup back onto the road. "And why are you telling me now?"

"Because we're not home yet. You could turn my sweet girl around and head into town."

Keats panted in my ear: yes-yes-yes.

"It's a crime scene, or at least part of a criminal investigation."

"I imagine Kellan's team has already picked it over with a fine-tooth comb. Isn't this where you normally go in to do the pet sweep?"

I actually laughed. She wasn't wrong. "What do you think my pets might find there?"

"Probably nothing. But what if the money is there? Believe it or not, I'd like to repay you."

"It's a bad idea," I said. "The kind of thing that drives Kellan nuts."

"I know, and I agree with him entirely." She gestured ahead with her index finger. "You can make a U-turn right there, darling."

———

FIFTEEN MINUTES later I tucked Buttercup into the bushes on a side street and we started walking toward Main Street.

"This might be the first time in my life I've regretted heels," Mom said, trying to keep up the pace Keats and Percy set. "If we have to run for it, just leave me to die and keep going."

"Do not make me laugh, Mom. This is serious business."

"I just want you to know I'm willing to make the ultimate sacrifice for you, my favorite child."

"Buttercup is your favorite child. You said so earlier."

"You're my favorite human child." Keats and Percy turned in unison and she told them, "You're my favorite grandchildren. Honestly, those boys of Daisy's... The first twins aren't so bad but the second ones, well, I've wondered if she drank too much during pregnancy. There was a time when Daisy got off track, you know."

"Mom. Golden rules of a break and enter? Stay alert. Stay focused. Stay quiet."

"It's not breaking and entering when you have a key," she said.

"I've tried that line on Kellan and apparently it is. It's most certainly trespassing."

"It's not trespassing when you have an open invitation to use said key. José wanted me to drop by after hours, but I never did. I only took a couple of private lessons, thank goodness, and in broad daylight."

"Okay, here's how this is going to go," I said. "We'll head up the fire escape and try the key there, first. You stick close behind me and do as I do. More importantly, you do as Keats says."

"What if I don't understand him?"

"Body language. You know the signs. If he gives a warning, we're out of there."

"What about Percy?" She held the back of my coat as I started up the stairs. "I don't understand him at all."

"Eyes and ears on Keats and you can't go wrong. Let me do the investigating."

"I do know the studio, Ivy."

"You don't know it like Keats knows it. You'll see."

I was worried about Mom's heels but she scaled the open, slatted metal stairs like a professional secret agent. When we got to the top, I reached behind me. "Key."

"Key," she said, putting it in my hand. I felt the cold

metal of the key... and something else. "Oh no," I said. A flick of the flashlight showed me a hard plastic key fob with a fuchsia heart in the middle that featured a gold letter D. It wasn't part of the original set Teri showed me. It looked like a knockoff, in fact. Or maybe a prototype that had inspired José.

"What?" Mom asked.

"Nothing. Nothing." I tried the key in the lock and it turned easily. "Quiet now. Keep away from the windows. If I turn on the flashlight anyone on the street could see us."

There was enough light from the big studio windows to explore the place. It had been cleared and dusted down thoroughly by the police.

Keats and Percy separated, each walking close to a wall until they met at the front window. Walking back through the center, Keats dropped his tail a bit to let me know it was a bust.

"There's still the foyer," Mom said, moving quickly on strangely silent heels. For someone who could thunder in stilettos she could move like a panther as well.

"Mom. Rules."

She dropped back to let Keats and Percy take the lead and fell in step behind me. Once we were in the foyer, the white tuft of Keats' tail shot up, followed only a second later by Percy's orange flag.

"There's something here," Mom said. "The boys say so."

"Let them find it. Faster that way." I turned on my phone light since there were no windows here. "Go, boys."

They circled the front desk where I had once spied on the yoga instructor's security feed. There was little left here beyond a few scraps of paper. The police had truly cleared the place. Keats sniffed the desk and sniffed some more, finally standing on his hind legs. Percy jumped on top of the polished wood and pried at the drawer with his claws. I used a gloved finger to help.

"There's nothing," Mom said, peering under my arm.

"There's something," I said, as Percy climbed right into the drawer. He did that twisty thing cats do and squeezed himself into the size of a paper clip so he could fit in a space far too small. "Percy, let me," I said, easing the drawer off its runners. That gave him more room to scrabble, and then came a clatter on hardwood. Keats darted under the desk and grabbed something. There was a moment of triumph as Percy emerged, and both tails rose. But then there was a simultaneous hiss and growl.

"Oh no," Mom whispered. "That means trouble."

"Which way?" I asked Keats. One white paw came up in a point. "The back door."

"Take the front then," Mom whispered. "Lights out, darling."

She seemed to fly down the stairs ahead of me, barely making a sound, and reached the bottom at the same time as the boys.

I unlatched the front door, poked my head out, and said, "Clear."

All four of us tried to leave at once and the Laurel and Hardy moment would have been comical had I not been scared out of my wits.

My hand shook as I locked the door and signaled them to start running. Mom went around the corner with Percy, but Keats waited. He mumbled something that sounded like, "Hoof it!"

Soon we were all racing down the side street, and by the time we reached Buttercup, Mom was in the lead. She pulled out another key, unlocked the passenger door and let the pets inside.

"Get in," she said, sliding the key over the roof. "Drive."

I did as she said, and once we'd circled enough of the back streets and alleys of Clover Grove to convince me we weren't being tailed, I pulled over and held up my palm.

"Spit it out, Keats."

He leaned between the seats and dropped another key fob into my hand. Navy blue, this time with a gold letter B.

"Oh, for goodness sake," Mom said. "That's it? Did Joe get a deal on these or what?"

CHAPTER NINETEEN

I was walking up the front stairs after my morning chores when two police SUVs pulled into the parking area. Jilly stepped out the front door in her flannel pajamas and a thick wool sweater, carrying two cups of coffee. She knew I had a story to tell but we hadn't yet had a private moment. Probably wouldn't now, judging by Keats' posture. His tail gave a hopeful wag and then drifted down ever so slowly.

"Bad news?" Jilly asked, handing me a mug of coffee. "The tail says so."

"It does." I tipped hot coffee into my mouth. "But the sirens aren't on."

"There's that," she agreed.

Early on in our tenure, we both got terribly anxious when the police arrived. Now my heart still accelerated, but there was as much excitement over seeing my boyfriend as dread over seeing Chief Harper. Regardless, there was no reason not to enjoy a good cup of coffee. No matter which of the two Kellans arrived, caffeine couldn't hurt.

Asher jumped out of his car first. He gave us a wave, flashed white teeth, and jogged to the camelid pasture.

Normally Alvina would be at the fence before he got there, but today she was in a corner alone. Drama and the others were pacing along the fence like a gang of thugs, which they pretty much were. My sweet girl didn't belong with them anymore but I didn't know what else to do with her. She needed company but hadn't shown much interest in any of the other animals. I'd given her a separate pen the day before and rotated sheep, goats, Archie the calf, and even Florence the blind mare in and out of there. The alpaca continued to huddle on her own and eventually I put her back with the thugs. Senna, the vet, assured me my girl would snap out of this funk eventually, but I wasn't convinced.

My brother wasn't, either. He raced up and down flapping his arms and then upped his game with a handstand and cartwheels. All to no avail. Finally he climbed the fence, waving his baton warningly at the thugs, and went over to pat the alpaca. She leaned her head into his chest and stood there, motionless.

"I'm worried about Asher's other girlfriend," Jilly said. "What else can we do to cheer her up?"

"Asher," I called. "Try singing. Remember what Cori said."

"Do I have to?"

"Just try it. She's depressed."

Asher stepped away from Alvina and sang, "When the Saints Come Marching In."

She lifted her head slightly and seemed to focus on him for the first time.

"Keep going," Jilly called. "It's working."

With Jilly's encouragement, his voice got stronger and he began marching up and down inside the enclosure, brandishing his club at the thugs to keep them from blindsiding him.

Slowly but surely, Alvina started marching along with him. It was far from a dance but her head was up and she was moving.

Setting my coffee on the railing, I applauded. "Go, Asher. Go, Asher."

Mom came out on the porch, too. She was already dressed in a fitted red suit that had been altered to show off her trim figure and great legs. Her faux alligator pumps matched perfectly and I looked at them differently today. Admiringly. The woman was stealth in stilettos and I wouldn't underestimate her again.

"Why isn't Kellan coming up to the house?" she asked. The way she kept smoothing her suit told me she was nervous.

"Good question. Maybe he's on the phone," I said, chugging the rest of my coffee before it could cool completely. "I'll go down and see."

"Shall I come along?" Mom asked. "Just in case?"

Jilly stared at her curiously. "What's going on? Which one of you got on Chief Hottie's bad side?"

Mom and I pointed at each other and then laughed.

"We don't know that he knows," Mom said, unbuttoning and rebuttoning her jacket. "Perhaps nothing. Remember what I told you, Ivy. Say nothing unless it's a direct question. I've been watching police procedurals lately."

"Yeah, but Chief Hottie is also Chief Boyfriend," Jilly reminded her. "Ivy needs to walk a fine line, Dahlia."

Mom looked down and smirked. "She'd do better in a nice pair of heels."

"A barnyard hazard," I said. "Stay there, Mom. Keats and I are going in."

Kellan got out of the car before we reached it and crossed his arms over the open door. "Morning, Ms. Galloway."

Ah. Chief Harper it was.

"Good morning, Chief. Could I get you a cup of coffee?"

"No, thanks. I'll take your full report right here."

"Which report is that?" I asked, watching Percy creep into the SUV. Keats stayed by my side, tail swishing ingratiatingly. It was rare that he showed Kellan such respect. Chief Boyfriend must be pretty mad.

"I believe you broke into the dance studio last night before we'd completed our investigation."

"It's not breaking in when you've got a key." The line hadn't worked before but it was worth another try.

"We've covered this ground." He scuffed his black boot on the nearly frozen earth. "It's trespassing. And more important, I've asked you time and again not to sully my crime scenes."

"How do you know it was even me?" I asked. "Was there a security feed?"

I hoped there was, because then we might find out who came in after us.

Kellan held out his phone to show me a set of footprints on the dirty hardwood floors of the studio. "I'd know those footprints anywhere. Because I see them everywhere they shouldn't be."

I examined the photo. "You don't know they're mine. Every homesteader in town wears these boots."

He glanced down at my boots. "Possibly, but they're larger than average."

"Big feet are a big help in manure management. Keep me steady."

For a second I thought he was going to smile but instead, he flicked his finger and then showed me another photo.

Paw prints. One larger set, one tiny set.

"I believe these belong to detectives Keats and Percy?"

Suddenly he lurched forward and his chin hit the car door as Percy leapt off the driver's seat and onto Kellan's head. Before he could react, the cat stepped down onto his shoulder and assumed the parrot pose.

"Oh Percy, that's so disrespectful," I said.

"Evading the chief of police's questions is also disrespectful," Kellan said. "We're supposed to be more open about things, Ivy. That's what we discussed on your porch swing a few weeks ago."

He was right, but I was finding it harder than I expected when the farm was threatened. I trusted Kellan and knew he was stellar at his job, but I also trusted my own instincts, and more importantly, my brilliant sheepdog's. It would take time to break down those barriers. Where my farm's welfare was concerned, Mom was right: I was emotionally unavailable.

I continued to squirm away from his questions. "You can compare the prints on your coat to the ones in your photo, I suppose. Unless Detective Percy cares to confess."

Percy kneaded Kellan's shoulder, purring loudly.

"I'll take that noise as confirmation," Kellan said. "And Keats' posture screams guilty, I'm afraid. I'm glad you at least took Jilly along. You're quite blasé about risking her welfare, but two is definitely safer than one."

I pressed my lips together, remembering Mom's words. No direct question, no direct answer.

"The paw prints were all over the front desk and the drawer was off the tracks," he said. "Care to explain?"

"I gave Detective Percy a hand with that. He thought there was buried treasure inside but got himself twisted up. I was trying to set him free when we heard someone coming in the back way and left through the front."

"Ivy!" The ironic humor in his voice vanished. "Why didn't you call me?"

"Because I didn't want to get in trouble. Like I am right now. We got out okay, locked the door and ran back to the car." I gestured to the porch where Mom and Jilly stood watching. "We're good."

He closed his eyes for a second. "You're good. Well, that's nice to hear because the person who came in behind you left the back door wide open. Who knows what could have happened next? A neighbor called to let me know."

"Did you find their prints?" I asked, eagerly. Too eagerly, because he pulled the phone away. "I wondered if someone followed me from Hazel's."

"Nothing clear. Whoever it was used a broom to cover their tracks."

"Huh. I'll have to remember that tip."

"Ivy," Kellan said, "what aren't you telling me?"

"Well, the culture revival project launch was a great success," I said. "When I was out back getting some air, I overheard Ryan Snopes and Tish Ramsey arguing again." I gave him the details and he took notes on his phone, managing not to dislodge Percy. "Detective Keats once again offered his view that those two are bad news. His hackles were, like... poof." I made a big circle around my head with my hands. "An eruption of fur. Pompeii all over again."

Now Kellan's lip twitched and he leaned very carefully over the door to eye Keats, whose tail rose and swished harder. The toxic black cloud was passing to expose Chief Hottie, which warmed my world on this cold day.

There was a crunch of gravel behind us and Mom called out, "Good morning, Chief Harper. I just wanted to apologize. It was my idea and I take full responsibility."

"Apologize?" Kellan asked. "For what?"

Mom stopped dead and then put her heels into reverse.

"For not offering you coffee, of course. Let me go right back in and get you a cup."

"Stop right there, Ms. Galloway," he said, checking his phone. "Are you telling me these prints are yours?"

Mom came back for a closer look at the photo. Confronted with a direct question, she had to follow her own rules. More or less. "They very well could be, Chief Harper. My feet are quite tiny and it's a terrible challenge to find nice shoes. You can't imagine."

"I can't. Nor can I imagine why Ivy would take you to a crime scene when you're under orders to stay here at the inn. I granted you leave to go to the Bingham Manor, not trespass on your old stomping grounds."

"I had an open invitation, Chief. José told me to come and go as I liked. I never did, of course. Men are so quick to take you for granted when you do things like that." She blinked a few times. "Men like Joe Barker, anyway."

"I'll ask you to surrender your key to the studio, Ms. Galloway."

"Of course. I'll go up and get it now."

"Take your time. Ivy and I have more to discuss."

"Can we walk, at least?" I asked. "It's so chilly this morning."

He gave a barely perceptible nod and moved gently away from the car before shutting the door. For some reason, he allowed Percy to stay where he was, and the cat continued to knead as we moved slowly to the camelid pasture. Finally Kellan turned to me again and two sets of eyes stared at me, angry blue and eerie green.

"Look, I know you want some freedom to take action when the farm is threatened," he said. "I try to allow for that, although it grates on me no end. It's bad enough when you and Jilly go off half-cocked, and worse still when Edna Evans is involved. But Dahlia? Seriously, Ivy, that is going to get you both killed, and perhaps others, too."

"You'd be surprised," I said. "She was actually very good. She listened and she outran me. It was a bit embarrassing."

"What if you were seen?"

"But we weren't seen."

"Dahlia is hard to miss. She's always in flaming red and heels."

I nodded. "Dressing up is her armor and right now she feels so ashamed about being conned. It brought back the trauma of my deadbeat father, who apparently cheated repeatedly before leaving us penniless and pitied by all."

Kellan and Percy blinked in unison. "I didn't know," he said. "I'm sorry."

"I didn't really know either, till last night. That's why I fell for her ploy. She wanted to see for herself if Joe had stashed the cash there." I watched Keats sidle up behind Kellan and shook my head at him. With claws so close to Kellan's handsome face, the fun might come at a price. "Actually, she wanted to see if Keats could find it."

"And did he?"

I shook my head. "The cash wasn't there. I suppose he'd already moved it along to the next town he was planning to bilk."

"If he had, we haven't been able to trace it. It may well still be around here, since many women paid in cash. But I'd thank you to let me conduct my own search. And for heaven's sake, leave Dahlia out of it. If she's that rattled she could be even more irrational than usual."

"I'll do my best, Chief. But she's at loose ends and the women inside are picking on her. She really needs to be distracted at the salon."

"Maybe," he said. "But only if you tell me—"

He didn't get a chance to finish the question before Percy turned green eyes toward the lane. Keats' tail beat steadily as a lime green van pulled in.

"Here comes my latest rescue," I said.

"Another one? You're going to need a bigger boat, Ivy," he said. "What is it this time?"

"Not sure. I had to say yes, no questions asked, in exchange for the intel we got about that politician in Dorset Hills. You remember. That great lead I shared with you right away."

"The dead end, you mean," Kellan said. "You're paying a high price for a bum lead."

"It's temporary. Cori told me to stop getting so attached to rescues."

"Well, for once Cori and I agree on something."

"I heard that," Cori said, hopping out of the van. "I cannot wait to hear which one of my brilliant ideas the Clover Grove constabulary endorses."

"If you told Ivy to ease up on the rescues, I heartily endorse that. She has a heavy load here."

Cori shook her index finger at him, managing to flash a little orange in the bargain. "You misunderstand. I said Ivy needs to stop getting so attached to rescues. They need to come and then go sometimes to make room for new ones. The farm is a clearing house."

"Like laundering rescues," Kellan said.

"Exactly." She tipped her head, and her sharp brown eyes appraised him. "We understand each other. Because of that I can compliment your new look. If anyone can pull off the pirate-parrot thing, it's you."

Bridget came around the van. "Cori, there's a reason we don't come here often. And you're taunting him now."

"And there's the other reason, taunting the llamas," Cori

said, orange middle now in full flash. "Hey, get out of there, Officer Smiley. Someone could get hurt."

Asher ignored her and continued strutting with Alvina. She'd picked up the pace considerably as he sang, "Walk Like a Man," complete with falsetto.

Even Cori grinned when she heard it. Then she walked around the van, warning us with an upraised palm to stay where we were. She slid behind the wheel and reversed quickly to the empty pasture Charlie had modified the day before. The fence was now eight feet high with screening at eye level.

Hopping out again, she opened the gate and then the rear door of the van. Bridget jogged over and they both went inside. I heard an unearthly squawk that sounded very much like the dragon I'd predicted. Or at least the dragon of movies.

"What was that?" Asher said, climbing the fence and running toward them.

"Stay back, Ash," I called. "It's a new rescue."

He started to back away and tripped over a stone, arms flailing just as Cori emerged with her arms full of the biggest bird I'd ever seen. It was taller than she was.

"Oh no, it's an ostrich," Kellan said. "Those things can kill."

The bird saw Asher flailing and started to struggle. Cori lost her grip and suddenly the new arrival was loose and on the move.

"Keats," Cori called. "Bring it in."

Keats tried. He darted and dodged, but the big bird's movements were erratic and completely foreign.

Cori beckoned all of us. "Fan out slowly, folks. No sudden moves. This bird can go thirty miles per hour, so we've got to surround her and press forward gently to the gate. Got it?"

We did exactly as we were told. With our arms all outstretched there wasn't much of a gap the bird could squeeze through and Keats patrolled the outside. I could feel all of us collectively holding our breath as we closed in.

The bird was practically in the doorway when the wild card played itself. Percy jumped down from Kellan's shoulder and charged. The bird dashed away, then turned and charged toward Kellan. He stepped aside lightly and called, "Ash!"

Just as the bird passed, Kellan tackled it. Well, tackled was too strong a word. He ducked his head and grabbed the bird around the middle and Asher joined him. I expected the terrified creature to peck and claw them but it went limp as they carried it into the pen. They set it down and moved like lightning to get out of there.

Kellan latched the gate and when he turned, something foul was running down his coat and uniformed pant legs. It was the largest splotch of bird poop I'd ever seen.

"Oh my," Cori said. "That's gonna stain. It's one reason I'm not a fan of the big birds."

"Cori, you can't leave me with an ostrich," I said. "I haven't a clue how to handle one and Keats doesn't either. It'll freeze out here."

She waved the glove. "First, it's not an ostrich and I hope I never have to rescue one because they're bigger, meaner and virtually untameable. This is an adolescent emu and quite a sweetheart once you get to know her. She was raised in an overcrowded pen so she'll need company." She snapped her gloves at Keats. "Bring the alpaca."

"Alvina? No, she's depressed," I said.

"She didn't look depressed prancing with your brother,

but a new friend will cheer her up. I have the feeling they'll be perfect together."

"That thing will not be perfect. Not ever," Kellan muttered.

"Trust me," Cori said.

"Not ever," he muttered again as she walked over to unlatch the gate to the camelid pasture. Alvina waltzed right out and over to Asher, who patted her neck.

Keats' service wasn't necessary as Asher escorted Alvina to the new pasture, and cautiously unlatched the door. She walked right in and began circling the big bird cautiously.

"You'd better check her toes, Ivy," Cori said. "She's favouring one."

"I'm not checking that bird's toes," I said. "Are you crazy?"

Cori looked at me like I was the crazy one. "I meant Alvina."

To my eye, the alpaca was moving just fine as she circled the bird, trying to suss her out. Finally the bird jumped and flapped. Alvina waited a beat, and then she jumped and bucked. Soon the two were chasing each other around the enclosure, one in the lead and then the other. It did my heart good to see my girl having fun again.

"See?" Cori said, turning to walk back to the van. "All in a day's rescue work."

"Thank you," Bridget told me. "It really is temporary, I promise."

Cori hummed "Walk Like a Man" as she jumped into the passenger seat and rolled down the window. "Chief Harper," she called, using his proper title for the first time. "I've got some intel for you on a nasty piece of work who's moved from our jurisdiction to yours."

"I'm all ears," he said.

"This place is all ears." She pointed at the porch, where most of the guests had lined up to watch the bird action. Then she held her glove to her head to symbolize a phone. "Call me."

For once, there was no orange middle finger.

CHAPTER TWENTY

Mom and I were both out of sorts when we landed in Bloomers later that morning. I was disgruntled over having to stay with her when I wanted to continue my investigation, and I certainly wasn't happy about having a new emu under my care that came with her own elaborate set of instructions at an already busy time. I sat in the corner of the salon surfing emu-rearing websites while Mom complained about being babysat by her youngest child.

"Mom, can we just make the best of it? Iris wanted the morning off and fair enough. She's been carrying the weight here lately and she's understandably worried about finances."

Mom pouted as she prepared her workstation. "Well, if I'd known José was a scammer I might have used my straight edge differently."

I looked up from my phone. "No murder jokes. As if people don't gossip enough about us."

"My theory is that if they're going to talk we might as well make it interesting for them."

"I don't share your theory. I've got an inn to run and once these guests leave, I'll be hunting for customers."

"Turn the place into one of those true-life murder attractions," Mom suggested. "People love that stuff."

I glared at her. "How about we just don't speak for awhile? Here comes Wayne Flagg, your favorite customer. Forget I'm even here."

"I could forget better if you'd sit in the back."

"Not gonna happen. We need to keep track of the action."

The "we" included both Keats and Percy, who were sitting on the ledge of the wide front windows. Eventually a good portion of the Clover Grove populace would pass and Keats would let me know if anything interesting cropped up. For the moment, he was surprisingly happy to see Wayne Flagg, one of Mom's first and most loyal customers. Wayne's word of mouth had brought a constant stream of men for her classic barbershop shave, including Joe Barker, unfortunately.

"Hey, Keats," Wayne said, as the dog jumped down to frisk around him. "I think he's finally warming up to me, Ivy. He never bothered with me before."

"We're all happy to be getting back to regular business," Mom said. "I'm so pleased you could make our standing appointment, Wayne."

I lapsed into silence, watching as she moved into her routine with practiced ease. In moments, Wayne was horizontal in the chair, face wrapped in fragrant hot towels, with just a couple of gaps for his nose and mouth.

"I missed this, Dahlia. Men like to be pampered too, I guess."

"Of course," she said, gradually perking up as she worked her magic. "Men don't get spoiled enough at home."

"Especially old bachelors like me," he said. "I rescued a dog recently to make sure someone's happy to see me."

Mom laughed. "Wonderful idea. Gets you out, too."

"Sure does. I walk that hound five times a day, all over town. Now it's dark so early you can get a look inside at how people live. That's why I wasn't surprised José ran into trouble."

Keats' tail lifted into an exclamation mark and I signaled to Mom to keep Wayne chatting. She nodded and picked up her little steamer. "Why do you say that, Wayne?"

"The private lessons. Every night it was a new lady. Blonde, brunette, redheads, gray and silver. What surprised me was how quickly they learned. The first time it was all stop-and-start but after a few sessions, some got really good. I ended up staying to watch the show."

Mom gave a tinkly, fake laugh that set off my alarms, but Wayne wasn't as sensitive. "I never saw you there, Dahlia. That's why I was surprised you got caught up in all this."

"I joined the afternoon group classes when I could get away from here," she said. "It was wonderful exercise."

Wayne waited a few beats before going on. "Sometimes there was less dancing and more gazing. That's when I'd leave because it felt like peeping rather than spectating. There hasn't been anything like ballroom dancing in Clover Grove before."

"It was nice while it lasted," Mom agreed. "Maybe some people took it too seriously, though. Maybe they hoped José would settle down."

The white towel bobbed in agreement. "I think he may have led women on. He was all over some of them, I'm sorry to say. You're too savvy for that, Dahlia."

"Oh, yes," she said, directing perfumed steam at his face. "That wasn't my first rhumba, Wayne. I'm afraid that lovely new lady from the bookstore café may have fallen for him."

I held up a hand to slow her roll. If she led him too far and too fast, she'd expose her game.

"Laurene Pedal. I saw her there, for sure. Nice lady. Too bad she always smells like cheese."

"Lots of other ladies talked about José," Mom prompted.

"Some of them surprised me," Wayne said. "Like Mabel Halliday. She seems like she has a head on her shoulders but there she was, spinning around looking happy as a lark. I guess some of the store owners couldn't get away during the day. Or maybe they didn't want to embarrass themselves in class."

"It's dreadfully awkward at the beginning," Mom said, and I nodded.

"The funniest was—" He stopped. "No, I shouldn't say it. You know how things get around."

"What's said under the towel stays under the towel," Mom said. "Completely anonymous."

"Well, the one to watch was Heddy Langman. Four left feet and arms like an octopus. She was all over José like white on rice."

Mom's hand steamer tipped up and sent a gust at the ceiling. "Heddy? How fun."

Heddy Langman and Mom had a rivalry going way back that recently blew up. Now, the sisters Langman slung mud on the Galloway name at every turn.

"Poor Heddy thought she was special, but there was only one gal he was crazy about as far as I could tell. Never got a good look at her, though."

"Younger, no doubt," Mom said, with a hint of bitterness.

She'd lost focus on her interrogation, but Keats hadn't. His tail had wagged slowly throughout the conversation but picked up the pace now. Something in Wayne's voice tipped him off that this was important.

"Don't think so. But she always wore a pink hat so I couldn't tell. I really think he fancied ladies your age or older," Wayne said. "I respected that about him. That red-headed firecracker was the only young girl—the one Ryan Snopes just booted."

"Well, I hope the police find the lady in the pink hat," Mom said. "She might have clues about what happened."

"Danced like a dream," Wayne said, and his voice took on a dreamy note. "Made even this old guy wish for the galas of his youth. We don't do that here anymore."

"Maybe it's time to revive the formals," Mom said. "As part of the culture project. And you can find the lady in the pink hat."

He laughed. "Dahlia, I saw your skills at the recital and you're the first one I'll ask. I've got more feet than Heddy Langman."

"But fewer arms, thank goodness," Mom purred. "Always a perfect gentleman."

With that, she whisked off the towels and the spell broke. Wayne's face flushed, either from the heat or because he'd said too much, and he enjoyed the rest of his shave in relative silence.

After Mom saw him to the door, she turned the closed sign and snapped her fingers.

Keats and Percy were at her side immediately but I didn't move. "What?"

"You heard the man," she said. "Heddy Langman was all over José like an octopus, so she knows something and we're going to find out."

"Mom, we promised Kellan to stay right here."

"I deserve a lunch break and I pick up my salad at the shop right beside The Langman Legacy antiques store. If we

were to run into the sisters by accident, what could Kellan
say?"

"Plenty. He could say plenty."

"You said one of those key fobs had a letter H, so Heddy
was probably José's backer. Maybe Kaye too, for all we know.
Those sisters could easily have taken him down together."

I checked in again with Keats before heaving myself off
the seat. "Okay. But promise me you'll keep a civil tongue.
You let your emotions get in the way of interrogation. You
could have done more with Wayne, but you got your back up
because of Heddy."

"I did fine for a beginner, Ivy Rose. One way we're
different is that I cut myself some slack when I'm learning.
You're always so hard on yourself and it holds you back."

I followed her out the door and let her lock up behind
me. "I wonder how that happened?"

"My fault, I'm sure. Nature or nurture, we moms always
wear it. Perhaps you'll find out yourself one day if you and
the chief can stop bickering and get on with it. I had four kids
by your age. Asher was a bonus, and you were a shock." She
caught herself. "A delightful shock, but a shock just the
same."

I could barely keep up with her as we covered the two
blocks to The Langman Legacy. Why had I seemingly inher-
ited her negative traits instead of her ability to put on a show
of strength to the world even when she didn't feel it? Why
couldn't I wear a smart red suit and pumps and tackle the
social alligators with flash instead of meeting my opponents
in the mud and manure?

"It stinks," I muttered and Keats circled back to shove
his ears under my hand. He gave me an injection of
courage and I reached into my coat to pull up the straps of
my overalls. No one could see them but it was easier to take

on the world when you knew your pants wouldn't fall down.

"Ivy." Mom clicked even faster. "Stop ruminating. I learned long ago that it doesn't help one bit. You know what does?"

"Stilettos?" I asked, clomping along behind her.

"That, and an unyielding belief you can bounce back from anything." She stopped outside The Langman Legacy and stared up. "I've done it, darling, and so have you."

I nodded. "It just gets hard sometimes."

"No one ever promised it would be easy, especially in Clover Grove. You do it for your kids."

"Kids?"

"The fur kids you have and the human ones to come. When I pass, I want you six to be able to say, 'She went down kicking and looked good doing it.'"

I laughed out loud. "You can count on that."

"In the meantime, I'll give you plenty to talk about among yourselves. My own parents were very dull. Unre-markable. I'm sorry you never met them but you probably wouldn't remember if you had."

"That doesn't give you a free pass to act like a lunatic today. Let me ask the questions, okay?"

"Of course. I'm learning more from you every day." She waited another beat and then said, "Door, please. I need to make an entrance."

She certainly did that. Kaye and Heddy Langman both flinched and then frowned when they saw Mom strut inside. I had to pick my way carefully through the precious old china and glassware but Mom moved with sinuous elegance.

"Darlings," she said. "How good to see you both. You look wonderful!"

Neither Kaye nor Heddy looked particularly well. Their

sensible hair was limp and their lines deeper than when I saw them last only weeks ago.

"Dahlia." Kaye's voice was withering despite the forced smile. "You look very tired. Understandable, given what you went through."

Mom stood a little taller and smiled a little harder. "What so many of us went through. It really was tragic, wasn't it?"

"It didn't affect us as it did you, I'm sure," Kaye said.

The defiant glint in her eye told me otherwise. Percy slipped behind the counter without their noticing and leapt lightly onto the shelf holding the cash register. He caught my eye and then tapped the orange key fob till it swung. The gilt H sparkled under the overhead light. Joe Barker must not have minded a human octopus as much as Wayne suggested.

Tapping her fingers on the counter's glass overlay, Mom tipped her head. "Come now, ladies. We've known each other since the cradle. Ivy, did you know Heddy and I were born within days of each other and shared the hospital nursery?"

"I didn't, no. There's much to be said for a long friendship. You'll forgive each other anything, I'm sure."

Heddy tapped the glass from her side. "I'm not sure I can forgive your mother for sending us into a dumpster chasing collectibles that never existed. I still smell trash in my nightmares."

"That was after you trapped me in my own salon, ladies," Mom said. "Two against one. I could have pressed charges. Chief Harper said so."

A lie, but one that deflated the sisters. "We only wanted to buy the collectible," Kaye said. "And pay a fair price, too."

"In the end you got more than one," I pointed out. "I put in a good word for you with Hazel Bingham."

"What do you want, Ivy?" Kaye asked. "You're only here if you want something we're not selling."

"The truth, that's all," I said. "We know Heddy and José Batista were very close and wondered exactly how much money she invested in his studio."

Kaye turned quickly to her sister. "You didn't."

Heddy's sallow cheeks turned blotchy. "Just a little of my own money. Nothing from the business."

"I heard you were a huge backer," I said. "José apparently gave special tokens to his A team."

Mom took out a compact and freshened her lipstick, letting her fuchsia key fob dangle from her fingers.

Heddy backed away, blocking her own key fob from her sister's notice. "It was just a little start-up coin," she said, more to her sister than us. "He promised to repay me with interest."

"He did well with you two," I said. "Because I heard Kaye contributed generously as well."

"I most certainly did not invest in his studio," Kaye said. Her eyes darted around and when she spotted Percy, she grabbed a feather duster and tried to flush him down off the shelves. He just went higher and strolled along the side wall, where the most valuable items sat on display. Then he sat down and wrapped his plumy tail around his paws, staring at me.

Heddy followed my gaze, and then said, "Where's the safe?"

"Which safe?" Kaye asked, too quickly.

"The antique safe Dad left us. It's been in our family for generations. Kaye, tell me you didn't sell it to José Batista."

"I did not sell Dad's safe to José."

"She *gave* it to him, free of charge," Mom said. "He could

be very persuasive, as we all know. How much was the safe worth?"

"It was priceless. At least to me," Heddy said. "I can't believe you let that man dance off with it."

"Ah, Heddy, take comfort in the fact you were among his favorites," Mom said. "Cash trumped all."

Kaye pressed her lips together for a long moment. "Ladies, we'll have to ask you to leave with your menagerie. We're closing early today."

"A family meeting, no doubt," Mom said. "I dread those like nothing else."

"Oh, Mom," I said, snapping my fingers for Percy. "You adore being called on the carpet by your loved ones."

Mom gave the Langmans a gay wave. "Delivering them was easier, believe me. Even Ivy, who came into the world with fists raised. They had to winch her out with forceps. I knew then and there it was my last."

"But not David's," Heddy said, with a nasty smile. "Or so we heard."

The shot about my father hit home. Mom didn't flinch but Keats leaned into her leg.

I stepped in front of her. "Good riddance to bad garbage, as the old saying goes." I glanced around the shop. "Of course, one woman's trash is another's treasure. Take care, ladies."

CHAPTER TWENTY-ONE

My sisters arrived en masse that evening to entertain the guests so that Jilly and I could get away to check out some of the first culture revival sessions. As part of the project's executive team, we wanted to make sure all went well.

Iris gathered the restless dance troupe near the fireplace and started to deliver her talk about hill country history. Within minutes, Poppy horned in with stories about her life as a roadie for a well-known band, and the guests clamored for salacious backstage gossip.

"Poppy is going to pay for that," I said, as we drove toward town. "I feel a family meeting coming on."

"It wasn't nice to steal Iris' thunder," Jilly said. "But for our purposes it worked well. The guests were so distracted they didn't even notice us leave." Keats tried to insinuate himself into her lap but she pushed his paws away. "Sorry, buddy. I'm on official duty as a culture rep tonight. Better stay clean. That goes for you, too, Percy," she added. "We know you're under there."

"I'm surprised Mabel and Teri set up their sessions so quickly," I said. "And on the same night, too."

"Competition. These nights can bring in business and the season of giving is fast upon us."

"All's fair in love and art, I guess." I was surprised and pleased I had to park blocks away because Main Street was packed with cars. "We're off to a good start."

At Mabel's Mutts, we walked through the store and joined a group of about 20 in the back room. Three people were sitting at potter's wheels while Mabel perched at another, explaining how to throw a clay pot. One of the potters-in-training was none other than Edna Evans, who was wearing coveralls instead of her usual camouflage.

I bent over and whispered, "What are you doing here?"

"Playing with clay. What does it look like?" Edna was using both hands to shape a mound of clay as the wheel spun. "If you won't include me in your investigations, I'll do my own."

"I'm just trying to—"

"No explanation necessary." She lifted a clay-covered hand. "I can see you find Dahlia's company preferable to mine. But I question your taste and your common sense. Do you think she's going to save you when the chips are down?"

Edna's pot collapsed suddenly and she watched the gray lump go round and around.

"She might try," I said, trying to keep a straight face.

"If your mother found you under attack on a manure pile, she'd excuse herself for a quick facial and hope for the best."

"You're missing the point, here, Edna. I'm trying to keep Mom out of trouble, not the other way around. When the chips are down, I know *you* have my back and I appreciate it."

Sighing, she dampened her hands and tried shaping the

pot again. "Can you tell me what we're looking for tonight? Because you know I'm neither crafty nor a joiner."

"Me either," I said. "How about we make a quick pit stop at Teri's and then hit the hobby farm session at Grub? Now that's something we can get behind."

Edna relinquished her wheel to the next eager participant. While she cleaned up, I took Jilly out to the front of the store to show her the ceramic version of Clover Grove at Christmas.

She gasped in childlike delight when she saw the little farm, and said, "Oh Ivy, we really must have it."

"It's not for sale." The voice behind us belonged to Alf Halliday, Mabel's husband. "Not till after Boxing Day."

"Oh, what a shame, but I understand completely," Jilly said, ever the diplomat. "You want to maintain the town's integrity."

"Someone has to," he muttered. "I remember when it wasn't so hard to do."

"Alf," Mabel said, coming through the curtain. "Let Ivy buy the farm if she wants to."

Jilly and I looked at each other and giggled at her choice of words.

"I'm happy to wait till Boxing Day, Mabel," I said. "Especially since I already have my miniature Keats. I noticed there's a little hook on the back so I can hang him from my very first Christmas tree. Maybe you could find time to squeeze in a miniature Percy as well."

"That I can do," she said. "I take special orders for special friends."

"Next year I'll enjoy the farm all the more. This is the kind of thing you bring out every year and treasure."

She beamed at me before turning to her husband. "Honey, we really could use the money."

His thin lips pressed together. "Yes, we could. Thanks to you. But we need to invest your time wisely."

Mabel glared at him but her smile returned quickly. "He'd prefer me to put the time into making new product rather than offering classes. My thinking is that people will see my work tonight and remember it when it comes time to buy gifts."

"They will," I said. "That's the double win with the culture project. We get to learn and have fun, and local businesses and organizations can benefit, too."

"You two will bring this community together in spite of itself," Mabel said. "No one else has been able to do that."

Her husband gave a little snort. "Murders aren't exactly the glue that binds."

I glanced down and saw Keats' ruff was rising and his tail didn't have a nice thing to say about Alf Halliday, either.

"Alf, could you go check on our guests?" Mabel said. "That clay can make a terrible mess if we're not careful."

When he was out of earshot, she apologized. "He's really not been himself lately."

"Come out to the farm when all this blows over," I said. "It'll inspire you to new heights."

"Join us for Thanksgiving dinner," Jilly said. "I'm cooking for a crowd."

"You are?" I said. "First I've heard of it."

"Just decided this moment. Seeing Mabel's pretty little farm put me in the festive spirit."

"Then my work here is done," Mabel said, laughing as Edna joined us.

"Thank you for a useful experiment, Mabel," Edna said. "It's never a bad idea for a survivalist to know how to make crockery."

TERI MASON WAS WEARING a caftan that looked like a rainbow when we slipped into Hill Country Designs.

Another 20 people—all women—were sitting around folding tables, heads bent as they created jewelry from metal, stone and pretty bits and bobs Teri had made herself. Moments of intense focus were followed by excited chatter as participants shared their work with each other.

Edna circled the room and everyone fell silent. She'd probably vaccinated all of these women at one time. There was a clatter as some beads hit the floor.

Keats raised his paw and pointed at Kevin Breen, Teri's boyfriend, who was sitting behind the counter playing with his phone. Teri knelt beside him and the dog's ears flicked back and forth in a move I hadn't seen before. It was nice he still had surprises for me, but I didn't know what he was saying.

Perhaps that was because he wasn't saying it to *me*. Teri seemed to know exactly what he meant because she sighed. "Yeah, buddy. Gotcha. It's curtain time."

Keats panted yes-yes-yes, and gently touched his nose to her cheek.

"That's rare," I told Teri. "The nose knows."

"Very rare," Jilly echoed. "Keats wants the very best for his family friends."

Teri gave his chatty ears a stroke and then stood up. "Well, this family friend is going to listen to the dog and do what's needed." She gestured around the room. "But not tonight. Tonight's about meeting new people and sharing my craft. I've sold quite a few pieces and already have sign-ups for the next class."

Jilly smiled and nodded, well satisfied with our project so

far. "I wish we could stay and play, but Ivy's determined to hit the session at Grub."

"Simon promised to talk about exotic birds," I said. "I can't miss it."

"Teri," Kevin called. "The wifi's down. Can you run upstairs and reboot?"

"Oh, I can boot and reboot," Teri whispered. "There are worse things than being single."

"Talk to the owners of your one-of-a-kind key fobs," I said. "Plenty of broken hearts over those hearts."

Her shudder said it all. She hated that her art had been sullied in a shameless scam. "Have you found all the owners? Any closer to answers?"

"Not close enough," I said. "But Kellan might be. He's not as free with his information as I am with mine."

Jilly gave a snort. "Yeah, you're all about full disclosure."

"I totally am! I just pick my timing." I grinned at her. "Saying too much too soon has a way of getting me sidelined."

"And keeping you on the right side of the manure," Teri suggested.

"I have Keats, Jilly and Percy for that."

"And Edna. She's the real powerhouse," Jilly said.

The powerhouse was leaning on the end of the counter staring at Teri's boyfriend. "Young man," she said. "Have I ever vaccinated you?"

"Uh, no," he said.

"Well, how about you run upstairs yourself to reboot the wifi and let Teri work? Or I'll give you a tetanus shot right now. I always keep a hypodermic in my bag. You never know when you might fall on a rusty earring."

Kevin slid out from behind the counter, keeping his back to Edna, and then bolted upstairs.

Teri covered her mouth and then laughed, as Edna joined us. "Oh my gosh, you just saved me a lot of trouble, Edna. I bet he's collecting his things now."

"Life's too short to put up with that," Edna said. "Ivy can tell you that my standards for men have always been very high. All I had to do was ask myself, 'Could you stand being stuck in a bunker with this man after the apocalypse?' It weeded men out very quickly."

"I'd love to be stuck in a bunker with Kellan after the zombie apocalypse," I said.

Edna frowned. "Zombies aren't real, Ivy, but plenty of monsters are. Shall we keep looking for the one at large?"

She flicked her fingers at Keats and he led the way to the door without hesitation. Since he didn't take directions from just anyone, that was the moment I accepted Edna truly was part of the squad.

I LEFT Keats and Percy curled up in a pile of fleecy blankets when we parked outside Grub. We couldn't stay as long as we might like with them waiting, but I didn't trust Gregor not to take a bead on Keats, let alone Percy.

The crowd inside was bigger than the other two combined. That was mainly because both genders were equally represented. The other sessions had been almost entirely women.

Simon had moved quite a few pallets to make room for the guests and set up a table in front of the cash register. He and Anne sat on it now, holding hands and swinging their legs. The two volleyed questions back and forth according to their expertise. Anne knew hens inside and out, as well as most small animals including the rare ones. Simon, on the other hand, could talk about cows and other livestock until, well, the cows came home.

"Ivy Galloway," he called as we walked in. "Let's give her a hand, folks. This woman is raising the profile of the hobby farm in Clover Grove. Hannah Pemberton picked up the flag but Ivy is the one running with it. Every time Town Council turns a blind eye to your exotic animals, keep in mind that Ivy's blazing the trail."

A smattering of people clapped, but Simon wasn't satisfied. "Folks, I insist. As you well know, I've seen hundreds of people come and go in this community and I've rarely seen someone so committed to animal welfare. So if you can't clap for Ivy... well, I'm calling out Gregor."

A laugh broke the tension and more people clapped. Simon let go of his wife's hand and clapped louder than anyone. Anne followed suit, beaming at me.

"Those two would survive the zombie apocalypse," I whispered to Edna.

She nodded. "Survivors. Both of them. Takes one to know one."

People asked so many questions that I couldn't get a word in edgewise about the new emu before it was time to head back to Keats and Percy.

Simon saw me buttoning up my coat and waved me over. "Sorry, Ivy, it's a hot crowd," he said. "We'll have to catch up on emus another day."

"No problem," I said. "I'm so happy about the turnout."

Anne squeezed my arm. "Honey, the rest of your order is under the counter. Grab it on your way out."

I circled around them and poked into a couple of bags until I found the new water heater for the henhouse and a coat for Keats that was likely to go over like a lead balloon. There was also an automatic feeder for the barn cats, who still refused to come inside. I knew they were warm and dry, but it still bothered me. The least I could do was offer them free food 24/7. They'd earned it by ridding the barn of rodents in record time.

"Got it?" Simon asked, leaning over the counter.

"Yeah." I stared around. "There's still something missing, but my mind's gone blank."

"I'll double check tomorrow and swing by if there is," he said. "Then we can talk emus without interruption. Just know it's a hardy bird and can handle the cold."

I heaved a sigh of relief. "This critter's got me a little worried, I must admit."

Anne joined us. "If anyone can handle it, you can, Ivy. Simon was right about you setting the gold standard for hobby farms in our region."

She grabbed my hand in her right and her husband's in her left and I felt a sudden infusion of energy where my confidence had been ebbing. It wasn't like a shot of Keats, but I'd take what I could get.

"That circle of love was a bit much," Edna said, as we walked out to the car. "Verging on tie-dye hippie love-ins, which incidentally, I'm old enough to remember."

"I think they're adorable," Jilly said. "I hope that—"

I waited for her to say something sweet about my brother but Edna wasn't as patient.

"In the case of an apocalypse, zombie or otherwise, there would be precious little time for love-ins. Or procreation for that matter. People of your generation don't seem to understand the basics of survivalism."

"Luckily we have you to teach us," I said, as she waited for me to unlock the passenger door. It was assumed, by both Edna and Jilly, that the latter would take a back seat on team outings.

"Let's start by throwing some pots together," Jilly said from the back seat. "You really seemed to nail that, Edna."

"Very funny, Jillian," Edna said. "You're going to need that sense of humor when you're stuck in a bunker with Asher Galloway."

CHAPTER TWENTY-TWO

The Palais Royale in Dorset Hills was the closest thing to a ballroom in all of hill country. It had once been part of a resort hotel that had long since been turned into condos in Dog Town's climb to the top of the tourist map. Even the ruthless former mayor couldn't find backing to destroy the old dancehall, however, and an investor had renovated the place for private events. That investor was rumored to be James Pemberton, Hannah's equally generous brother, who owned a fair bit of property along the lakefront in Dorset Hills. Remi Malone, a founding member of the Rescue Mafia and a fundraiser for the hospital foundation, managed the space and threw regular events to benefit animal charities.

Tonight's gala for pet rescue was an old-time formal dance, which coincided nicely with my guests' desperate need to leave the inn. Kellan agreed, so long as they were well chaperoned, and Asher raised his hand as Jilly's date. Edna, Iris and Violet also volunteered, which left me free to leave early. Kellan wasn't available and I wasn't in the least interested. Besides, with all the chaperones at the ball, someone needed to be at home to play Cinderella.

Still, I caved to Jilly's pressure to make an appearance for the Mafia's sake. I felt like I'd already contributed to their cause this week by opening my doors to a very large bird. That's why I felt justified in boycotting fancy dress. Instead I wore the only suit I'd saved from my corporate days and paired it with my dressier work boots.

I expected Edna Evans to back me in the formalwear boycott. Instead she was in a deep purple dress with more than a few sequins, a lovely, long scarf, and patent leather Mary Janes. Her hair was freshly colored and permed.

"What happens if the zombie uprising takes place tonight?" I said. "You'll be caught in a frock."

"Far from it," she said. "That's why I rode with Jilly in Buttercup and gave up the chance to mock your driving in the truck. It was a sacrifice, but it allowed me to stash my go-kit in the trunk. I need to know I can be in fatigues and a helmet in minutes if necessary." She glanced down. "There's a time and place for work boots, Ivy, and it isn't at the Palais Royale."

I refused to feel either ashamed or embarrassed. Mom had already tried and if she failed, Edna had no hope. "I'm not staying long. There's no one guarding the farm and I couldn't bring Keats. Strike one and strike two."

"Strike three is that Kellan is working, I suppose," Edna said. "You make an effort for him."

"We make an effort for each other... between murders." I sat down beside her at one of the big round tables. "I can't even think about dancing while the killer is still out there." I shivered, although I was still wearing my coat. "Or in here, for that matter. Still, it's a relief to know my guests can finally enjoy themselves. Making people happy is harder than I expected."

Edna laughed. "It's something I never had to worry about. Life is too short to cater to the whims of adults who want to dress like ice skaters indoors."

"Right? It's enough trouble catering to the whims of my eccentric animals."

A waiter delivered a grapefruit martini to Edna. It was one of her few luxuries, and she sipped it slowly. "Do you regret leaving human resources?" she asked.

"Never." The answer came out with enough force to satisfy Edna. "But after being miserable in HR, maybe it should have occurred to me that I don't like people that much. Hence hospitality is a stretch."

She stared at me over her glasses. "If you're looking for a hug, you've come to the wrong place, Ivy. Most days you know full well you've found your calling." Smoothing her sequins, she added, "It's not like you to be so self-indulgent."

"Sure it is. Keats just takes my edge off." I chugged half my soda and gave a little burp. "I'm frustrated that I haven't figured out who killed Joe Barker. Maybe I just got lucky before."

"Four times?" Edna asked. "Possibly. Or maybe you're getting lazy. I bet you know all you need to know right now. Time to put it together."

Collin came over and offered Edna his hand with a little bow. I expected her to burn him with caustic words, but she got up straight away. "Why thank you, young man. I'm a bit rusty, but I'll take a spin." As she followed him onto the dance floor, she called back, "Lazy people aren't welcome in my bunker, Ivy."

"Isn't this the worst?" Cori Hogan said, taking Edna's seat. "I'm only doing it for the dogs."

She was wearing a sharp black suit and dressy boots that could get her through an urgent rescue if necessary. But she hadn't given up the gloves of attitude. The "formal" version was a lightweight knit with some sheen, the orange flares less garish. Even Cori would compromise if it served animals.

Bridget took the seat on my other side and suddenly I felt better. It wasn't a hug but it was something even better. Acceptance. They didn't care how I dressed. They measured me only in relation to my caring for animals. On that scale I knew I ranked pretty high.

"You know what you need?" Bridget said. "Alpaca therapy."

She pulled out her phone and played some clips from the video shoot. There was very little of José in her footage, so it didn't remind me of my inadequacies as a sleuth. I took the phone out of her hand and watched Alvina whirl and twirl for my brother on that clear sunny day, when life felt full of promise.

Handing back the phone, I stared into space. "What?" Cori said.

"I don't know. Something." I couldn't put my finger on it. "I wish Keats were here."

"I wish Beau were here, too," Bridget said. "I only have half a brain without him."

"Same," I said.

"That's where we differ," Cori said. "Without Clem, my border collie, I am still the smartest person in the room. With him, I'm three times as smart." She flexed her gloves. "It's all in the math, folks."

I was still laughing when Collin returned, and offered a little bow to me. Edna was spinning with James now, keeping up very well for a woman of any age. I liked that they'd treated our senior companion with such respect, so I surprised myself by accepting.

"Ooh," Cori said. "Chief Hottie's gonna be jealous."

I grinned at her as I got up. "He's allowed to dance on the job too if he likes. All in a day's work."

"Dancing *is* work," Collin said, offering his arm as we went out to the floor. "The job is to make it look effortless."

"Collin, I'm wearing steel-toed boots. I could break your feet."

"Don't think about your boots." He tapped his temple. "It's all up here, Ivy. Just follow my lead and you'll forget everything else."

Wasn't going to happen. Nothing could stop my mind from spinning except for one dog whose mind spun constantly for me and gave me some downtime.

There were a few false starts. I kept trying to wrestle Collin for the lead as if he were my stubborn sow, Wilma. After I accepted my role as follower, it wasn't so bad. For a moment or two, I enjoyed the spangled light from the mirrored ball on the ceiling and smiled at the sight of Jilly trying to show Asher the steps.

"Focus and let go," Collin said.

"Aren't those contradictory?" I asked, as he maneuvered me skillfully around the floor. For him, it probably felt like driving Buttercup or worse, the truck. Especially when he had three accomplished partners waiting for their turn. Arlene, Stacia and Maeve were all enduring lesser dancers with stoic smiles.

"Not at all," he said. "Release your preconceptions of what you *should* do. Just focus and let go. Trust that all will unfold as it should."

His tone was soothing, almost hypnotic. Eventually I stopped thinking about my boots and started listening to the music, hearing the beats, *feeling* the beats. Collin whirled me round and around and we covered the entire dance floor many times over. Jilly's green eyes widened in shock, and then squeezed shut as my brother stepped on her.

Asher just needs to let go, I thought. Focus and let go. We weren't raised that way.

One song, two songs. We were well into the third when the trance broke. "Oh!" I said. "Collin, I have to go. It's bedtime for the animals."

"Just one more dance," he said. "You're a natural."

That was exactly what I needed to hear to keep backing away. Slowly at first. By the time I reached the parking lot, I was running.

CHAPTER TWENTY-THREE

"What's wrong?" Kellan's voice boomed over the speaker as I drove home.

"Nothing. I just needed to hear your voice. I thought if we talked, the truck wouldn't stall as much."

He laughed, and some of the tension drained out of me instantly. "You really do flatter me, Ivy."

"It's a compliment. To say my obstreperous truck likes your voice. You're the truck whisperer."

"Far from it," he said. "But hopefully I help the obstreperous truck's driver when she's had a hard night."

"That's just it," I said. "It wasn't hard. I danced with Collin."

"Am I supposed to be jealous? Because I'm not. I trust you."

"Good, because Collin is definitely not my type. More like my mom's type. But here's the thing, Kellan. While I was dancing with him... he actually *felt* like my type."

"Okay, now I'm slightly jealous. Satisfied?"

"No, no, no. What I'm saying is that I finally get what was going on with the women José swindled. This dancing thing... When you're with a master, it almost transports you. Collin isn't as skilled as José by his own admission. Yet I forgot about my work boots. I forgot about the emu. I even forgot about Keats for nearly ten minutes. That's gotta be a record."

Kellan was laughing again. "You wore work boots to the gala?"

"Well, yeah. You weren't there. I only dress up for you. Willingly, anyway. Sometimes under duress for my mom."

"Now I'm truly flattered." His voice deepened and sent a rush of sparks up my spine.

"Whoa. Whoa, chief. Turn down the smolder. Got no time for that till the killer's behind bars."

"You're right," he said. "But I'm sitting here with a pile of paperwork trying to put the pieces together and... I miss my girlfriend."

"I miss you, too. I'm sorry if I've stepped on *your* work boots lately, Kellan. The more times this murder thing happens, the more flustered I get, it seems. I want to grab all the clues and hoard them so I can fix it."

"It's okay," he said. "I know you tell me what I need to know anyway."

"By which point you've usually figured it out. Did you find the Langman's antique safe?"

"Not yet. But thanks to Percy we probably have the key for it when we do. I'm guessing B is for Barker. How about the mysterious N key fob? Any luck?"

"No, and it's annoying because I feel like I *should* know. That if I just turned around fast enough I'd find the truth standing right behind me."

He sighed. "I've ruled out everyone, pretty much. There's not a scrap of evidence to suggest the dancers did it, and the locals look clean, too. I'm going to need to go further afield."

"That'll take forever. Can you at least send the dancers home?"

"Tomorrow," he said. "I'm going over everything one last time tonight."

"Switch on your intuition," I said. "And I will, too."

"Right. Let's focus and let go."

"Hey! That's what Collin said about dancing."

"Makes sense. Dancing is somewhat intuitive too. Let's see where that takes us and talk tomorrow."

I was almost at the farm now and starting to feel a little anxious. "Can I call you when I get home? There's no one else there. I mean, except Keats, Percy and fifty animals, including a large jumpy bird."

"You can call me anytime, all the time. If I'm not in the middle of a takedown, I'll talk you through whatever you need."

I laughed. "You got it. Thanks to you, I haven't stalled once."

"Keep it that way. And when you're finished with the critters, lock yourself inside until Asher gets there."

"And Edna," I said. "I feel safe with her."

There was a long pause at the other end. "I can't say I'm flattered about being on par with Edna Evans, octogenarian and noted wing nut."

"She's not as crazy as she used to be. Or maybe I'm crazier than I used to be. But I find her in normal range now."

He snorted. "She wears fatigues, drives an ATV and likes using a crossbow."

"You need friends like that in your bunker. She's learning to throw pots now so that we can have crockery after the zombie apocalypse."

"Is that right? Well, I'll never make crockery for you, Ivy. I want you to know my limitations."

"But you'll bring so much more to the bunker," I said. "And I bet you could use a crossbow."

"Wouldn't mind giving it a try," he said. "Take down a zombie or two."

"That's the spirit. You're definitely my first choice for the bunker."

"Before Keats?" he asked, slyly.

"Keats and I count as one unit," I said. "So you're my first choice. Alongside Percy."

"I still beat the pig and the emu," he said.

"There's no room in the bunker for them, unfortunately. Or Drama and the thugs. Luckily zombies only eat human brains, so the critters will be safe."

"Is that true?" He sounded startled. "I mean, in zombie lore? Obviously it's not true for real."

"Totally true. That's why Edna has a helmet in Buttercup's trunk right now."

He sighed and I could tell he was shaking his head. "Flirting with you is always interesting. Gotta keep my wits about me."

"Bye, Chief," I said, turning into my lane.

"Call me to tell me you're safe inside."

"Promise."

KEATS FROLICKED as if I'd been gone for two days instead of two hours. He raced ahead of me to the barn with Percy, two furry streaks that had no problem focusing and letting go. They were always fully, intently present in the moment. Well, mostly. Keats had more angst than most dogs and he probably siphoned most of that out of me. Thankfully, being a working dog, he never lacked for constructive outlets.

There wasn't much work left in the barn, and I vowed to avoid the temptation to work the manure. Tonight, I'd keep last call short and get a good night's sleep to bolster my intuition.

Starting my rounds in the barn, I checked on food, water and bedding, and offered treats that appealed to each stall's residents. Then I popped into the henhouse to make sure the new water heater was working. The small peeps and the ruffle of feathers soothed my nerves.

The respite was momentary, however, because the next stop was the shed Charlie had cleared out to hold the emu overnight. The big bird apparently didn't mind the cold, but I had to witness that for myself over the coming days. Besides, she was quite a climber and I really didn't want to be chasing a bird that could clock 30 mph through the bush in the dark. The golf cart didn't go that fast even on smooth terrain.

She—if indeed it was a female—was sitting comfortably on a stack of old blankets in the corner and didn't move as I gave her a wave. I had decided not to name her. One thing I'd learned is that naming a creature basically replaced the "temporary" sign. The name made it mine. And as much as I wanted to throw open our doors to all rescues, there had to be limits. As Charlie always said, they had to fit together in a cohesive community. Adding a calf was no big deal. Adding an exotic bird was another matter entirely. It would be fun to see a huge emu egg, though. And even more fun to see her run. Full out, like she would in her native Australia. The greyhound of the bird world.

"I should get an ATV," I mused aloud, after locking the barn. Keats, Percy and I made our way to the last stop, the camelid pasture. "Edna loves hers and it would be way better than a golf cart in a zombie uprising. A golf cart isn't a survivalist vehicle. It's preppy rather than prepper."

Keats offered a skeptical blue eye.

"Right," I said. "Focus and let go. There's no such thing as zombies. But it doesn't hurt to be ready."

Alvina broke away from the others and came to the fence to visit me—something she hadn't done since the night of the murder. Her interest was more about the biscuit tin under my arm but I'd take what I could get. I practically shoved the first treat into her mouth, expecting Drama and the thugs to swarm over and try to mug me. The donkeys were always ravenous and would chew off my sleeve given half a chance. Tonight they stayed in their corner, probably plotting something nefarious. The two donkeys had formed a V with the llamas behind them. It was an interesting formation because I'd put my money on Drama any night of the week.

"What's up with the thugs, girl?" I said. "Are they hazing you for being the fan favorite?" She accepted another biscuit, but when I tried to pat her neck, she pulled away. "Fine. Play hard to get. You're a one-man woman." She tried to reach under my arm for the tin and I backed away. "But I hear you like Frankie Valli and the Four Seasons, just like Mom always did, and I can carry a tune." I hummed "Walk Like a Man" and she stared at me with her big eyes. In this case I was probably imagining the skepticism. "Fine, I'm not a man and I'm not walking away from you or even Drama and the thugs. You got me there."

Keats gave a little whine to hustle me along. Already I'd been out here longer than I intended. But if Alvina was cracking open a little, I didn't want to rush her.

"How about this one instead?" I started singing, "Can't Take My Eyes Off You."

Alvina took a step closer and rested her chin on the

fence. I held my ground. Maybe she was going to spit on me, but it was a risk I was willing to take. I kept singing and she started to hum, too. Her happy sound. I gave her another biscuit and her big brown eyes locked on mine as she crunched. We were having a moment—a communion—for the very first time. My heart filled with joy and I did a little spin and waved my free hand. If I could get her to dance with me, it would make a stinky week smell a whole lot sweeter.

Keats gave another whine, this one more urgent.

"Cut me some slack, buddy," I said. "Alvina and I are bonding."

When I glanced down, his eyes weren't on us but the lane. My singing had drowned out the sound of an approaching vehicle.

"They're home already?" I said. "Bummer. I wanted an hour alone by the fire."

But it wasn't Buttercup or the sedan Asher had borrowed for the evening. It was a construction grade pickup truck even larger than mine. Alvina gave a guttural grunt behind me and Keats growled as the driver pulled into the parking lot and rolled down the window.

I was starting to worry when Simon Rezek stuck his curly head out and grinned.

"Hey, Ivy. Good to see you getting your groove on with your livestock. Maybe we should cover that in my hobby farm sessions."

I laughed. "Hey, Simon. Can't a girl bust some moves with her alpaca in the dark without getting a reputation?"

"Not in this town," he said. "All you have to do is breathe wrong to get a rep."

"Sadly, I have good reason to know. Dancing in the dark with my animals is the least of the gossip."

"People don't realize how just a few words can slice someone's reputation to bits," he said.

I walked to the truck. "One minor indiscretion and you're digging yourself out of a very deep hole for the rest of your life. It's easier to move."

"Some holes are too deep," he said, leaning back in his seat. "They can ruin your business. Your health. Your marriage. Everything. If you moved, the hole would follow."

Obviously we weren't talking just about me anymore. "You okay, Simon? If someone's been trash-talking you, I'll send my pig after them. You're the third nicest guy in Clover Grove."

"Third?" His teeth gleamed in the dark truck.

"After Kellan and Asher. Maybe tied with Charlie. Gotta keep him on my side now that there's an emu to worry about."

"You're good people, Ivy," he said. "Shame about what's happened here." His hand gestured around the farm. "You deserved better."

"Aw, thanks, Simon. We all hit a rough patch now and then. It'll pass."

"Hope you're right," he said.

"What brings you here so late?" I asked.

He rattled a bag on the passenger seat and then handed it to me. "Still owed you these."

I looked in the bag and saw the missing toe trimmers from my list. "You didn't have to rush, but thanks. Alvina has a split nail and I thought that might be why she wasn't dancing. Turns out she was just depressed. The emu perked her up."

Simon laughed and it sounded oddly hollow floating above me on the cold air as he looked around. "Where is everybody?"

"Fundraising gala over in Dorset Hills. My guests are dancing their blues away, and they're not alone. There seems to be a real appetite for ballroom dance. Both men were talking about setting up shop in the studio."

"What?" Simon sounded alarmed. "We don't need that ballroom crap around here. Didn't the last loser prove that?"

Keats was leaning against my shin and I could feel, rather than hear, his nonstop, rolling growl. "You got Gregor in the back seat?" I asked.

Simon shook his head. "Sent him home with Anne. She doesn't like being alone these days."

"Yeah, me either." Not when my dog puffed to twice his normal size. Not when the blades on the tool in my hand fit the exact description of the murder weapon. And especially not when I'd seen my old clippers in Simon's hand in Bridget's video earlier in the evening. "In fact, I promised Kellan I'd go right inside and call him after singing Alvina a lullaby."

Alvina wasn't dozing off anytime soon. I could see her moving along the fence behind me and she let out a screech like I'd never heard before. Drama and the thugs started pacing in a restless circle.

"What's up with Alvina?" Simon asked, sweeping off his ever-present baseball cap. There was just enough light to show a sheen of perspiration on his balding head.

"I bet it's that split nail," I said, pulling the clippers out of the bag and starting to pry open the packaging. It was easier to break into a safe than sealed plastic like this. The shards were almost as sharp as the blades. "Maybe I'll trim it now. Don't let me keep you, Simon. Poor Anne's on her own."

He turned off the engine, opened the door and hopped out, replacing his hat as he did. "No worries, I'll give you a hand."

Oops. My strategy had backfired so badly that Keats wedged himself between my boots.

"Simon, your community spirit is showing," I said, smiling. "But Anne's always so kind to me and I refuse to keep you a second longer."

Leaving the door of the truck open and the headlights on, he started walking toward the camelid pasture. "Don't worry. Nan'll be fine with Gregor."

Glancing into the truck, I saw a key fob with a scarlet heart dangling from the ignition. The interior lights made the gold N glitter.

Nan. A pet name only Anne's nearest, dearest and most possessive knew. There was a pink hat on the passenger seat as well.

So she really did like to dance, after all.

CHAPTER TWENTY-FOUR

"On second thought, it would be silly to start trimming in the dark, Simon," I said. "It could do more harm than good. Better to tackle that in daylight."

"But I'm here now," he said. "A certified expert in alpaca nail trimming."

"There's certification for nail trimming?" I asked, just to keep the conversation light.

"Sure. You can get certified for anything on the Internet these days." He gave a grim chuckle. "You hold the light and I'll show you how it's done."

He held out his hand for the trimmers.

"I learn better by doing," I said, continuing to pry open the packaging. "You explain and I'll trim."

No way would I bend over and offer my head for a thump, though. I had to think fast.

"Fine, have it your way," he said. "Come on, now."

That's when I realized my boots hadn't moved. I was still standing near the truck with Keats between my feet.

"Simon, I have a bad habit of overreaching, especially when I'm tired. Kellan's always asking me to slow down and think about what I'm doing. So I'd really rather wait till tomorrow. Senna will be here and can train me. But thank you."

"Let's just get it done," he said. "I'm going in with or without you. I've got a utility knife."

Finally I started moving and Keats preceded me, belly low, hackles high. I couldn't let Simon and his utility knife go inside the pen with my animals. He might be armed with worse for all I knew. The feed store was licensed to sell firearms.

"I wouldn't, Simon. The donkeys are raring for a fight. Have been ever since... what happened to José."

"I don't know why they wouldn't just trample him," Simon said.

I stopped walking. "Pardon me?"

He turned back, grinning. "I mean, when I heard the story of how he climbed in here late at night. He was a drunk dancer, not an animal wrangler. You've got to have your wits about you when dealing with livestock, right?"

"Right. Which is why—"

"I'll get the gate," he said, plodding on.

As I followed, I finished prying the clippers out of the packaging and slipped them into my pocket. At the same time, I yanked out my phone and texted Kellan one word: help.

Then I hit the record button and turned on the phone light. The battery was low. Hopefully there was enough juice to get me through the next 10 or 15 minutes. That's how long it would take the cops to get here.

It was time to dance for my life.

Simon went inside the pasture and I loitered at the gate. Did I shut myself inside with him and trap the animals there, too? Or did I leave the gate open so they could escape, and risk them escaping and injuring themselves another way?

Keats whined and raised one paw in a point. Right! The pig poker. Normally I left the long wooden pole with its rusty brass hook near Wilma's pen, but since Drama had gotten so feisty with Keats, I'd started leaving it here. Now it was only a few yards away. If things got as bad as I feared they would, I could grab it from the inside and pull it over. Just having a shred of a plan made it possible for me to pull in a full breath. I was going to need oxygen to fuel my best brain cells if I hoped to talk my way through this.

"Let's go, Ivy," Simon said.

I let Keats into the pen and pulled the door closed, making sure it didn't quite latch. Keats glanced at me with his blue eye, confirming he noticed.

"Leave the dog outside," Simon said. "No reason for him to get hurt."

"No one's going to get hurt with a nail trim, are they? Otherwise we wouldn't be doing it."

His teeth gleamed in the light of my phone, and he turned his phone on, too. "Leave him if you like. It's just a precaution. You know how unpredictable animals can be."

I knew how unpredictable human animals could be as well. "Let's just get it done fast."

"Agreed." He said it too quickly and I knew exactly what *he* wanted to get done: kill me.

He knew I'd figured out what happened the night José died. My expression obviously gave me away when I saw the trimmers. What a terrible time for my normally reliable poker face to fail me.

He walked over to Alvina and she backed against the fence, eyes wide and terrified.

"She's scared, Simon," I said. "Maybe you could try dancing with her first to settle her down."

He turned quickly. "I don't dance, Ivy. Never did, never will. There's no place for that kind of thing in Clover Grove. It makes people lose their wits. In farm country, we can't afford to lose our wits."

I nodded. "No argument there. José was foolish trying his moves out here alone."

Simon continued to stare at me. I couldn't get a good look at his eyes but I knew they had the crazy gleam. I'd seen it before. I'd felt the vibes. The train had left the station and all I could do was keep it rolling before it zoomed off the tracks. Again.

"He was the worst kind of loser," Simon said. "He took advantage of women. Good women who lost their minds over his fancy footwork."

"I know. He scammed my mom out of some of my hard-earned savings," I said. "Every cent counts around here."

"Dahlia I'm not surprised about. She's the type to fall for a stupid ponytail."

"Well, she had plenty of company. Quite a few women in town contributed generously to José's start-up fund. It doesn't mean any funny business was going on, Simon."

"I saw what I saw," he said. "All I had to do was park outside his studio a couple of nights. Dancing like that goes nowhere good."

I leaned against the fence, easing slowly toward the pig pole. "I might have said the same thing till tonight. I took a spin under the mirror ball with a skilled dancer and it really did transport me for a few minutes. All the worries of my life —and there are many—faded away. That's when I understood why women wanted to keep José in town. It wasn't because they loved him or his ponytail."

"He gave them big ideas. Romantic ideas. That's not what life out here is all about. Like you said, every cent counts. Your reputation counts."

He swept off his hat again and swiped at his eyes with the sleeve of his coat. I didn't know if it was sweat or tears, but it was a chance to move a little further along the fence.

"I know, Simon. It's so gallant of you to think of the women who got taken for a ride. Luckily Anne didn't dance. She was safe from José's wiles."

I was trying to give him an out. To tell him I didn't suspect him. His heavy breathing paused for a second, and maybe he considered taking the escape route I offered.

"It doesn't matter if she did," he said. "If other people thought it was true."

"I've never heard Anne's name come up and I have access to insider information."

"Just a matter of time. You know what this town is like. She wore a pink hat to disguise herself. Like I wouldn't know that hat anywhere. I gave it to her."

"You and Anne have the kind of relationship everyone envies," I said. "You're best friends and business partners as well as husband and wife. We all want to be like you guys."

"It can all fall apart in a second," he said. "One minute your wife is holding your hand, the next she's handing over your retirement savings to a fancy dancer."

"Oh, Simon, if that happened to Anne, I'm so sorry. But you know full well it was just dancing. Just money. She'd never cheat on you."

"Just dancing... Just money..." He mimicked me. "Just disrespect and complete annihilation of my social standing." The baseball cap came off again, and this time I could see his face was streaked with both sweat and tears. "She gave him twenty grand and still holds my hand like it never happened."

"That's because it didn't mean anything to her. You can recover that money, I bet. The police are looking for an old safe."

He put his hat on crooked. "I got it from his apartment. Looks like an old piece of crap but I can't break into it, even with an axe."

"But you'll get there. And you can figure out a way to return the money to everyone. You'll be a hero."

"Ivy, you're a nice person. Too nice. Too gullible." He took a step toward me. "And way too nosy. That's what makes people need to kill you. I'm sorry."

"You're sorry people want to kill me?" I asked, lightly. I was almost at the pig pole. If I could keep him talking just a minute longer, I'd be able to grab it and haul it over. Then I'd run like heck and count on him to follow. Away from my animals.

"Yeah," he said. "And sorry I need to finish what others have failed to do."

"Kill me? Why on earth would you do that?"

"Because you know too much."

"Like I'd ever tell anyone about Anne. I like her, and I refuse to believe she did anything more than invest in a dance studio. People do worse every day."

"I've done worse," he said. "And you know it."

"Ah. So you're the one who ridded our town of a nasty pest? I should thank you."

"You should. But instead you'd tell your boyfriend."

"Women don't always share. Like you said. How about we just keep it a secret between us?

It was the wrong thing to say. The hitch in his breath told me so before he blurted, "No more secrets."

I raised my hand. "Okay, okay. If you're going to kill me, you might as well tell me how you lured José out here. I'm nosy, like you said."

"Easy. Texted him from Anne's phone. There was a string of messages where he called her 'his biggest patron' and 'his Nan.' No one ever called her that but me."

"That's how a conman works, Simon. They get personal details and exploit them."

His breathing hitched again, as if fighting back sobs. "Don't you get it? No one used that name but me. But she *let him*. She responded to his texts. Even if racy dancing was all that happened, she broke our trust. It can't ever come back."

"That's where you're wrong, Simon. People rebuild from worse all the time."

He shook his head over and over, as if trying to shake loose an image. I expected it was Nan in José's arms, gossamer hair flying as she spun away from the drudgery of this life.

"It didn't mean she didn't love you," I said. "She thought she'd get the money back soon, and with interest."

"Go ahead and take her side, Ivy. You know where that's getting you? Nowhere."

That's where he was wrong. It got me to the pig poker. But just as my hand touched the wooden pole, Simon lunged.

CHAPTER TWENTY-FIVE

I f I'd expected anything in that moment it would have
been for Keats to lunge, too. And my dog didn't let me
down. The problem was that for all his natural spring, he
couldn't launch far enough to inflict much damage to a large,
tall man. Keats was smart enough to know that and bide his
time by going for Simon's calves.

What I never expected was for Alvina to throw herself
into the fray. She was a sensitive beast, barely recovered from
the last crime committed in this pen by night. Maybe I'd
made an impression with my singing earlier, or maybe she
was tired of her turf being invaded. Either way, she let out a
strange, feral bray and moved in front before Simon could
reach me.

And then she did what an alpaca under pressure does:
she spit in his face. I had dropped my phone in my pocket to
grab the poker with both hands so I didn't have the pleasure
of seeing it happen. But I knew well enough what it felt like,
and smelled like, and based on his yelp, Simon's eyes had
been wide open to receive the blast. He hopped around,
trying to wipe his eyes and probably only rubbing it in more.

"Alvina, Keats, come," I yelled, starting to run for the gate while maneuvering the pig poker. I turned to see if she followed. Alvina wasn't used to commands and this girl danced to her own drummer.

Simon held his arms wide to block Alvina's path, and with his back to me, yelled, "Guess I'll hunt some big game before the small game. Alpaca goes down first. The dog second, and you third, Ivy."

"Not going to happen," I said, hauling back the pole. "Not that way."

Alvina let out another screech. She sounded terrified now. If I swung at Simon hard enough and he dodged, I could hit the alpaca.

Keats saw the dilemma. He ran as he never had before in a huge loop, bringing Drama Llama and the thugs across the pasture. When they got near the fence, Percy jumped onto Drama's back and held on like a bareback rodeo rider. His claws spurred Drama on, and the llama led his crew straight at Simon. At the last moment, Drama dodged. The redirect gave Percy a chance to leap onto the fence again. Simon spun out of reach in a move that was more like a ballroom dancer's than he'd ever care to know. The alpaca spit must have cleared from his eyes because he managed to clamber up the fence quite easily. I thought he'd go over... Make a run for the truck. Instead, as Drama and the thugs circled back, Simon did the stupidest thing I could imagine: he jumped on the fierce llama's back.

"No!" I yelled, holding the poker like a baseball bat in case I could get a swing at him. Drama bucked under the big man's weight. Simon managed to stay on. I'd heard he did rodeo work in his youth and he still had the skills, if the wrong animal. Llamas weren't built to carry a man that large.

"Leave my llama alone," I yelled.

"I couldn't get them to trample the dance king," Simon yelled. "But that's how you're going down, Ivy."

Keats had other plans. I turned to see him pulling at the gate from the bottom and Percy did the same from the top. It swung open and Drama Llama saw his opportunity. He gave a last buck and then bolted with the rest of his gang in pursuit.

A shriek rang out and I wondered if Simon had been thrown already. I hoped not. I wanted Drama to give him the thrill ride of a lifetime. Or deathtime, if that's what Fate had in mind. It was out of my hands now. All I could do was protect the animals.

Keats and Percy started to follow and I called them back. "Let him go, Keats. Get Alvina and we'll take his truck in case he comes back."

Keats hesitated, clearly itching to go after his man. Finally he circled the alpaca and she followed me out without a protest. My initial plan was to run her down to the barn, but by the time I unlocked it, got her inside, and ran back, Simon could be back and mowing me down. I didn't think he'd get far on Drama.

So I went with plan B.

Running to Simon's truck, I opened the back door of the cab. It was an awkward jump, but if Alvina would do it, a safer ride than the open bed at the back.

Keats gave her heel a little nip and she put her front legs up on the runner. I started to boost from behind, knowing she wasn't that heavy. She scrabbled and her bowels unleashed in the struggle. It wasn't her fault and incontinence was the least of our worries. Putting my shoulder into it, I got her inside and closed the door.

I saw a light in the pasture and said, "Get his phone, Keats."

Percy and I jumped in, and I already had the truck rolling slowly when Keats came back and catapulted right over my lap into the passenger seat. It was the biggest truck I'd ever been in, let alone driven. But I managed to get it in first gear and chugged forward.

"Hold on, everyone," I called, pulling the door closed. "Gonna be a bumpy ride."

I did a slow, wide U turn in the parking area and then nearly hit the clutch when I saw the lights bumping through the fields toward me.

I knew those lights. I just didn't know who was behind them.

"Should I stay or go?" I asked Keats, who had one white paw raised in a point.

His mouth opened and he panted ha-ha-ha.

I put the truck in neutral and waited till the headlights joined to reveal what Keats was laughing about.

Edna's ATV rolled into view, slower than I'd ever seen it move. Behind her, Simon Rezek stumbled at the end of a rope. His hands were cuffed and his mouth gagged by the scarf she'd worn earlier.

She jumped off, still wearing the purple sequinned dress. I got out of the truck to join her.

"Honestly, Ivy," she said, yanking pepper spray out of her coat pocket. "Can't you keep your trouble at home? I was pulling up to my house in a cab when this idiot rode by on your llama. I hopped on my vehicle and pursued till I got close enough to lasso him. Simon was spouting all kinds of madness so I knew what I was dealing with. Came right over to make sure you're okay."

"I'm okay. We're okay," I said, gesturing to the truck. Keats and Percy had already jumped down and Alvina's face was pressed to the rear window closest to us.

Edna started to laugh. "Did you stall that thing?"

I straightened my shoulders and adjusted my imaginary crown. "I did not."

"What was your plan, if you don't mind my asking?"

"Bringing my trouble to your house, of course. I was going to set Alvina up in your recliner while I waited for the police. She deserves the rest after what happened."

Edna smoothed her dress and shook her head. "Not in my recliner, Ivy Rose Galloway. Friendship has its limits."

"What are we going to do with Simon?" I asked.

The question was answered by the sound of sirens. The big man started to thrash at the end of his rope.

Edna aimed the pepper spray at him and said, "Don't make me come over there, Simon Rezek. Nothing would make me happier than to give you your final vaccination."

Keats frisked around her patent Mary Janes and Percy leapt onto my shoulder and then Edna's. Despite all that had happened, I smiled at the image Kellan would see as he pulled in. For better or worse, there would never be a dull moment in our relationship.

"I'VE BEEN LOOKING all over for you," Kellan said, joining me at the fence of the alpaca pasture where I stood in the darkness. "You okay?"

I nodded. "I couldn't bear to be around when Anne got here, so Edna and I left to round up Drama and the thugs." I gestured to the corner, where the llamas and the donkey grazed happily on their late night snack. "They made it all the way down to Huckleberry Marsh and then tried to turn back. The footing down there is treacherous at the best of times. So Edna lassoed them one by one and we towed them back."

Kellan grinned. "She can lasso, too?"

"Oh yes. Very useful when dealing with a zombie uprising. She apparently snagged Simon in one go."

He slung his arm around me and pulled me close. "I can't believe I'm saying this but... I want Edna Evans in my bunker. When the worst happens."

I buried my face in his coat and then pulled back. It smelled like he'd been at the wrong end of one of the animals, too. Now I got a whiff of my own medicine.

"Whew! You caught it bad, buddy."

He laughed. "When you rode off with Edna, Asher and I had to get Alvina out of the truck. He got the spit, I got the poop."

"Me too," I said. "The couple that stinks together stays together. I hope."

He hugged me tighter and shone his light over the field. Alvina left the feed and trotted toward us. "She seems fine. But will she ever dance again?"

"Time will tell." I stared up at him. "You heard the full confession?"

"Yep. Well done. The team's already collected the safe and in time all the women who care to step forward will get their money back."

"That's wonderful. What about Anne? Did she know Simon knew?"

Kellan shook his head. "She had no idea he'd realized the money was gone. She handled their finances and he never confronted her. Instead, he just assumed she was guilty of far more than she was. I don't think there was an affair. In fact, I don't think it went that far with anyone, as much as some women may have wished for more."

"Heddy Langman," I said.

"And others, including his dance troupe. Plenty of women wanted to be the one to pin this guy down forever."

"They wanted that fix. The magic of dance. It can hold people together for life, you know. There were lots of seniors at the gala tonight, glowing as if it were their very first waltz."

"I'm sorry I can't give that to you," he said. "Cops don't really dance. It sends the wrong message."

"Not out here," I said. "Not with an alpaca."

Alvina had joined us and was staring at Kellan in a way that said if he played his cards right, he could take over from Asher.

"Ivy, really? You want me to dance with Alvina now? After a night like this?"

I cued up my phone and cranked the volume on "December, 1963" and sang, "Oh, what a night..."

Kellan glared at me and shook his head. But then he gave a little jump that both Alvina and I took to be the start of his routine. When he looked down, however, I realized Keats had tried to hit my boyfriend's "on" button with a sharp nip.

"Fine," he said. "But only if you join me."

I hit pause and replay, set the phone on the fence post and took the hand he offered. We danced rather sedately at first, but as Alvina started matching our moves inside, I hit replay over and over and we hopped, twirled, and flailed until we were warm under the cool moon.

I did pirouette after pirouette until I was dizzy and sang, "Why'd it take so long to see the light?"

"Seemed so wrong but now it seems so right..." Kellan answered, offering a spectacular leap that Alvina mirrored.

Keats and Percy raced around in the frosty grass, and when Kellan and I finally fell into each other's arms again, laughing, Percy climbed the fence and landed on his shoulder.

"Watch out for our eyes, pal," I said. "Gotta keep them wide open around here."

Kellan straightened. "Do you think Edna saw all that?"

"Saw, filmed and planning to use as blackmail if necessary," I said. "She went home about an hour ago, so she had her equipment."

He sighed. "There goes my reputation."

"Oh, don't worry," I said, leading him to the house. "Give her back the crossbow you confiscated and this will all go away. She was complaining about being inadequately armed tonight."

"I can't do that," he said. "But if she buys another for the bunker and I don't hear about that or the dancing, well..."

I stood on tiptoe to kiss him. "Oh, what a night. I hope it never happens again. Except the dancing part."

"That part ended much too soon," he said, laughing as he balanced Percy and then let Keats herd us up the stairs.

CHAPTER TWENTY-SIX

The inn had never smelled so good. I drew in a breath for the count of seven and let it out again. Turkey, stuffing, cinnamon and so much more. Jilly had pulled out all the stops in preparing a spectacular Thanksgiving feast for our friends. My deep breaths were partly about cleansing all the typical farm smells, but mostly about the number of guests. In addition to our usual crew of family and friends, she'd invited Hazel Bingham and her nephew Michael, Mabel and her grumpy husband, Mandy McCain, Ryan Snopes, Laurene Pedal, Teri, Charlie and more she hadn't told me about yet.

Collin from the dance troupe was staying at the inn until he found a place in town. He was going to rebrand and reopen the dance studio—a bold move in a community that had a long memory. He'd planned to win people over by offering tap, ballet and modern dance classes to the kids first. The way in here was always through animals or children, so he might just pull it off.

"Go up and get dressed, Ivy," Mom said, coming into the kitchen. She was wearing an apron, as if there was any risk of her getting her red lace dress dirty from pitching in. Mom was allergic to domestic work and rarely pretended otherwise. With Mandy and Daisy on hand, there was no shortage of truly willing hands.

"I am dressed." I'd paired a nice sweater with my best jeans—the ones that only had a couple of small holes in the cuffs.

"There's a stain on your bum, young lady," Mom said. "And it's Thanksgiving. So take an extra shower, too."

"Fine. Whatever. It's so nice to feel accepted for who you are in your own home."

"Oh, boo-hoo," Poppy said. "Seems like you've forgotten to be thankful about receiving this home on a silver platter."

I stared at her. She'd died her hair brown again and when I looked around the kitchen, I realized we Galloway Girls looked like Russian nesting dolls, one just like the others. I was the tallest and Daisy the shortest—with Mom being shorter still—so we fit together in reverse order.

"You've got a point, Pops," I said. "I have more to be thankful for than ever this year. Including the fact that your hair is boring again."

"Girls, can we all get along for a few hours?" Daisy said. "Jilly's done a lot of work for us, and I am extremely thankful for that."

"This *is* getting along," I said, pushing open the kitchen door. "And I'm thankful for Jilly every day all day, and she knows that."

"Ditto, my friend," she said, stirring gravy and peeking into the stove at the same time. "Go if you're going because dinner's not far off."

"Keep an eye on Mom, Keats," I said as I left. "I don't trust her not to put the moves on Collin in front of Charlie and Michael, and it would be so tacky."

"I heard that," Mom called after me. "I'll be the very first to sign up for your Rotation 101 class when it launches, darling."

I gave everyone in the family room a wave as I passed and noticed a murmur starting once I'd gone up the stairs. What were they talking about? I wasn't thankful about having secrets being shared under my roof.

When I came back down twenty minutes later wearing a skirt and a cashmere cardigan that the wardrobe fairy had left on my bed, everyone was facing the door and there was a barely suppressed excitement. Keats stood out in front with his tail lashing, and he gave a loud woof that sounded like an announcement.

"What's going on?" I asked, stepping into the room.

The crowd parted and I saw that the antique oak sideboard Hannah had left behind had been cleared of vases and candles. In their place was the miniature village from Mabel's shop—not just the farm but the entire snow-capped town.

"For the inn?" I asked.

Mabel's face was wreathed in smiles. "For you, Keats, Jilly and Edna when she wants to come over and enjoy it."

"I thought you couldn't part with it yet," I said, glancing at her husband.

"They made us an offer we couldn't refuse," he said.

"Who's 'they'?" I asked.

"The association of women wronged by Joe Barker," Mom said, with a wry smile. "Nearly everyone pitched in—at least those who admitted to being taken for a ride."

"The fund far surpassed the cost of the village, so I'm adding to it as fast as I can," Mabel said. "Edna, your house is done, but I haven't found a mold for an ATV yet."

Edna, who was wearing another nice dress, looked quite

touched. I might have said her edges softened, but a tin of pepper spray poked out of her handbag.

"Well, I'm just thrilled," I said. "There really couldn't be a nicer gift, or a better way to start my own holiday tradition here at Runaway Farm. Thank you to the association of women wronged."

Jilly clapped from the kitchen doorway. "Time to sit down, everyone. Hurry, before my Potato Puff falls."

People dispersed with the speed only a good meal can cause, leaving me to admire my new town with Kellan.

"I wanted to buy the farm for you," he said, "but Alf wouldn't let me have it. I was thinking about applying a little cop pressure when the women intervened. Now, I've got to think of another gift. What do you get a girl who already has the whole town?"

"Nothing," I said, squeezing his hand. "I don't need a thing."

He stared at the tiny town. "It's quite something. There's the police station."

"And a little ceramic cop," I said, grinning. "Hot enough to melt the snow off his cap."

"Very funny." He picked up the little cop and moved him over to the ceramic farm. "He prefers being over here."

I moved the little cop to the camelid pasture. "Where he can dance with his alpaca friend. Poor Asher's slid from first place, now."

Once Kellan and I had broken through our inhibitions, we danced with Alvina often. She enjoyed it most when we danced together. Her kicks were higher, her spins faster and her bucks more enthusiastic. Now that she spent most of her time with the temporary emu, her mood was stable and upbeat. That said, Drama and the thugs had mellowed somewhat after their trip to Huckleberry Marsh. I figured they'd realized the grass wasn't always greener outside their pen.

Kellan gave me a hug and said, "I'm looking forward to our first Christmas together."

"Me too. Let's get the tallest tree we can find. And then we'll make a wish that there's never another murder in this charming town."

"Perfect."

"Ivy," Jilly called. "Time for the host to say grace."

Kellan and I drew apart and I gave a little scream. A monster was making his way through the ceramic town.

"Percy, off! Off!"

He stared at me with big green eyes and deliberately knocked over one building. Two. Then he pretended to scrape litter over one poor snowy soul in the town square beside the Christmas tree with its colored pinpricks of light.

Kellan blew out a long breath. "Far from me to get woo-woo, but is that cat trying to tell us something?"

I glanced down at Keats and his blue eye had an intensity I recognized.

"Well, he does like to bury the dead," I said, moving the cat. "But let's not think about it now." I led Kellan away and he craned backward trying to see what Percy had supposedly predicted. "We're trying to live in the present, remember?"

We took our places at either end of the table and everyone held hands as I said a quick, but heartfelt grace. The table was long—three tables together—so I couldn't easily keep track of everyone. But I noticed Hazel and Edna catching up on old times, and Teri Mason, who'd come alone, chatting quite happily to Collin.

"Oh, no," I muttered to Mom, who was seated beside me. "Is Poppy hitting on Ryan Snopes? Is that why she dyed her hair? He's rebounding from Tish."

"Let them have fun," Mom said. "I'll advise Poppy to get a strong rotation going so she doesn't overinvest. It'll be easier now that she looks... well, normal." She had a sip of wine. "All my girls are attractive, but Jilly is the fairest of them all."

"Why thank you," Jilly said, raising her glass. "I'm thankful to be an honorary Galloway."

"Let's do that thing," Asher said. "You know, where we all say what we're thankful for? Other families do that all the time."

"We're not other families," I said. "We keep things locked down."

"Not anymore," Jilly said, tapping a glass gently with a spoon to call for silence. "So I'll start: I'm thankful you all came today to be part of our family. Families you make are the very best."

Asher went next. "I'm thankful Ivy came home. And I'm really thankful she brought Jilly with her."

Everyone laughed and looked to me. But Mom's hand shot up.

"I'm thankful for red dye and my sewing machine," she said. And when everyone laughed harder, she looked surprised. "And for my children, of course."

"And...?" Daisy prompted.

"And my grandchildren," Mom added. She pointed at Asher and then at me. "And future grandchildren, if the universe is kind."

Blushing, Jilly gestured to me to break the tension.

I thought about it for a moment. How did I keep this short, yet meaningful? "I'm grateful that Jilly and Keats led me out of a life I didn't know I hated into one filled with adventure, family and more love than I could have ever imagined."

Kellan raised his glass and said, "I'm thankful for Ivy.

That part's simple. But also community. I came home for that and got so much more."

The food disappeared rather quickly as everyone took a turn sharing. There was laughter and tears in about equal measure.

Finally, as the parade of pies came out, I said, "Me again. Host gets to go twice. I'm thankful for my animals, particularly Alvina. She taught me to dance. To find the spark of joy even when things are hard. It's something we all need to do."

Everyone put down their cutlery and applauded. The moment was at risk of becoming saccharine, but Percy took it upon himself to burst the bubble by leaping onto the table and parading down the middle until he seized an abandoned turkey wing and departed as suddenly as he came.

"Better watch your emu," Asher said, getting up to follow the cat. "We have a predator in our midst."

"It's not my emu," I called after him. "It's temporary."

Kellan shook his head and sighed loudly. But when Percy landed on his shoulder a few minutes later, he didn't shoo him away, even as the cat left greasy paw prints on his nice shirt.

"Best holiday ever," I told Jilly, as she served me three types of pie without my asking. "Can't wait for Christmas."

Do you want to try my other mystery series?
The SECRET series that's hidden in plain sight?

Sign up for my newsletter at **ellenriggs.com/opt-in** to find out how you can read the first in the 11-book series for free. There's a little more romance, a lot less murder and plenty of heartwarming humor.... plus a large cast of mischievous mutts. My newsletter is full of funny stories and photos of my adorable dogs. Don't miss out!

While you're waiting on the next book, if you would be so kind as to leave a review of this one, that would be great. I appreciate the feedback and support. Reviews buoy my spirits and stoke the fires of creativity.

RUNAWAY FARM & INN RECIPES

Jilly's Fall-in-Love Beef Stroganoff

Ingredients

5 tbsp unsalted butter
3 shallots, thinly sliced (or about a cup of thinly sliced sweet onions)
Roasted garlic, optional (1-2 cloves)
1 lb mushrooms, thinly sliced
1 tbsp Dijon mustard
¼ cup white wine
2 tbsp all purpose flour
1 cup beef stock
½ cup sour cream
1 ½ lb beef tenderloin, cut into pieces, 3 X 1 X 1/8 inch (Strip loin steak is fine, too)
Salt and pepper

In a large saucepan over medium-high heat, melt 3 tbsp of butter. Add shallots or onions, and cook for about 10 minutes, stirring often, until caramelized. Add roasted garlic, if using.

Sprinkle in flour and stir constantly for about 2 minutes. Whisk in mustard and wine, and then continue cooking until liquid reduces by half.

Stir in stock and bring to a boil. Cook until thickened, about 2 minutes more. Stir in sour cream and remove pot from heat.

In a large skillet over high heat, melt remaining 2 tbsp of butter. Add beef and stir-fry until no pink remains, about 3 minutes. Reduce heat to low, stir in sauce and season to taste with salt and pepper.

Serve over cooked egg noodles or mashed potatoes and garnish with parsley.

Made in the USA
Las Vegas, NV
04 March 2022